MISSING

SPECIAL FORCES CADETS

CHRIS RYAN

SPECIAL FORCES CADETS

MISSING

HOT
KEY
BOOKS

First published in Great Britain in 2019 by
HOT KEY BOOKS
80–81 Wimpole St, London W1G 9RE
www.hotkeybooks.com

A CIP catalogue record for this book is available from the British Library.

ISBN: 978-1-4714-0782-6
also available as an ebook

3

This book is typeset using Atomik ePublisher
Printed and bound in Great Britain by Clays Ltd, Elcograf S.p.A.

Hot Key Books is an imprint of Bonnier Books UK
www.bonnierbooks.co.uk

1

Rebreather

'Hands up if you want to drown.'

The man asking the question had wavy black hair, a black beard and heavy eyebrows. His eyes were dark and so was his expression. His name was Hector, and the five teenagers standing in a line knew he wasn't joking. Nobody moved.

'Hands up if you want enemy snipers to locate you because bubbles of your breath reach the surface.'

Max Johnson looked beyond Hector to the still surface of the lake. It was March, and very cold. The water was inky. Tendrils of mist rose from it. He imagined gunmen with high-powered sniper rifles camouflaged in the scrub that covered the steep, rocky slopes on either side of the water.

He kept his arm, clad in a tight-fitting wetsuit, firmly down.

'Hands up if you want to risk coming to the surface too early because you've run out of oxygen.'

Max glanced left and right. His fellow cadets were watching Hector carefully. Lukas, a black boy from the gang-ridden streets of Compton, Los Angeles, wore his usual frown. Max had only recently learned that it didn't necessarily mean he was in a bad mood. Sami, a slender Syrian street kid, was shivering in the early-morning cold,

1

but trying not to let it show. Lili was Chinese. Her long black hair was pulled back from her face and she fixed Hector with a fierce, intelligent gaze. Nothing got past her. Abby, born and raised in a tough Northern Ireland prison, had pale skin, blue eyes, thick brown hair and a double cartilage piercing in her left ear. She looked moody. 'Hands up,' she muttered under her breath, 'if you'd rather go back to bed.'

'Button it,' Hector said.

'Ah, c'mon, Hector,' Abby replied. 'What is it, five thirty in the morning? We haven't even had breakfast yet.' She hugged her body. 'I'm freezing.'

This was precisely the wrong thing to say to Hector. Two months ago, Max, Lukas, Sami, Abby and Lili had been badged as Special Forces Cadets. The cadets were a secret team of young soldiers. They existed to perform missions where adult Special Forces would be too conspicuous. It meant they had to be hyper-fit, highly trained and prepared to endure almost any hardship.

'If you can't manage an early morning and a bit of weather, young lady, say the word,' Hector said.

'Ah, Hector.' Abby smiled at him. 'You're in the sweetest mood this morning. Did you have a lovely dream about making teenagers cry with exhaustion?'

Hector grunted. Abby was the only one who could talk to him like that. She was a charmer, in a blunt kind of way.

'So,' Hector continued, 'when we need to cross a body of water unobserved and we want to stay submerged for a substantial period of time, we use one of these.' He indicated five packs by the water's edge, each of them a mass of tubes and hard casing. 'These pieces of apparatus are called rebreathers. Rebreathers provide oxygen and remove carbon dioxide in an enclosed environment. So, unlike scuba-diving gear, no bubbles. The same technology is used in mine rescue, mountaineering, even in space. But today . . .' He turned and looked meaningfully towards the lake. 'Today, underwater.'

Max shivered. The water was not inviting.

'Your rebreathers can keep you under for up to six hours. I wouldn't recommend spending that long in these waters unless you want to contract hypothermia. Which you don't, by the way. Your objective this morning is to reach the far end of the lake without reappearing above the surface of the water.'

Max squinted. The far end of the lake was not visible.

'Distance, about one mile.'

Just a couple of months ago, Max would have found that a ludicrous instruction. But that was the old Max. The new Max, the Special Forces Cadet Max, had grown accustomed to being given seemingly impossible tasks and expected just to get on with them. As Hector never tired of saying: if Max wanted to be spoon-fed, he'd come to the wrong place.

'But it will be dark underwater,' Sami said. 'How do we know we're going the right way?'

Hector pointed to a separate pile of equipment. 'Swim boards,' he announced. 'You hold them in front of you while you're underwater. Each one has an illuminated compass and depth gauge. Regular Special Forces might also use a special underwater GPS system, but I'm not here to make life easier for you.'

'You don't say,' Abby muttered, earning herself another dark look from Hector. 'Ah well,' she said. 'I guess it beats sitting in a classroom learning Morse code.' The previous day, Abby had been vocal about Hector's insistence that they learn Morse, but her reluctance had had precisely zero effect on the Watcher.

'Where are Woody and Angel?' Max asked. For the past two months of intensive training, Woody and Angel had been their constant companions. Along with Hector and Martha – the stern, unsympathetic matron back at Valley House where they all lived – Woody and Angel were the cadets' Watchers. And they'd certainly been watching them. They had been on the range while the cadets practised their shooting skills. They had roared encouragement as the cadets ran up bleak mountainsides, on the verge of exhaustion. They had taught them navigation skills, survival skills, surveillance skills, how to drive, how to pick locks and how to move unseen around the countryside. They were like an elder brother and sister to each of the cadets, full of advice, support and friendship.

But today, there was no sign of them.

'In case you were wondering, Woody and Angel don't have to check in with you,' Hector said with a curl of his lip. Max was used to Hector treating him differently. More aggressively. He understood why – he and Hector had a complicated history – but that didn't make it easier. 'Get your rebreathers on and grab your swim boards. You'll be entering the water at two-minute intervals. Move.'

The rebreather was heavier than it looked. Max figured

this was because of the oxygen pack. He clipped the apparatus to his body and placed the mask over his face. It fitted tightly. Hector went around the cadets checking the equipment was properly fitted. He handed each of them a swim board. The compass at the front glowed only faintly in the grey morning light. Max knew it would be brighter in the murky water. He got his bearings: the far end of the lake was in a north-westerly direction. So long as he kept that trajectory when he was underwater, he should be okay . . .

'You first,' Hector told Max. The older man took him by the arm and forced him to the water's edge. The water was icy, even through Max's neoprene shoes. He knew better, however, than to appear reluctant. Steeling himself against the bitter cold, he waded into the water. Clutching his swim board, he dived like a salmon. The cold water knocked the air from his lungs. He found he was unable to control his breathing. He inhaled sharply as a matter of reflex. If he had not been wearing a rebreather, he would have a lungful of lake water. He breathed out slowly, trying to regulate himself. His heels were still splashing above the water. He kicked hard and plunged deeper, holding the swim board at arm's length.

The compass did indeed glow brighter underwater. Max saw he had already moved a few degrees off-course. He readjusted his direction as he continued to swim deeper into the lake. He knew that if he broke the surface at any point, Hector would make him repeat the exercise until he could do it properly. And as he moved further into the depths of the water, it struck him that Hector's plan was working.

Hector had tried to stop Max from joining the cadets. It was a weird way of trying to ensure Max's safety. Now Hector was going out of his way to ensure Max's training was as tough as it could be.

Train hard, Hector had told him, *fight easy.*

His movements were slow and difficult because of the cold. His whole body was like a block of ice, his extremities numb. He estimated that he was about ten metres deep. There was a faint glow of daylight up above, but his visibility in front was poor. He had to trust the compass on his swim board. Down here, there was no other way of navigating.

He swam through a shoal of tiny fish that darted off in different directions. He wondered how far he'd swum. It was almost impossible to tell as he had no real sense of how fast he was moving. He estimated he'd been underwater for seven or eight minutes. That meant the others would be in the lake by now. He suddenly felt competitive. They were all his friends, but that didn't mean he wanted any of them to beat him to the far end. He kicked harder.

The attack came out of nowhere. Three figures, black-clad and strong, came at him from left, right and front. He was paralysed with panic. Who were these attackers? How had they found out about the Special Forces Cadets? What did they want with him? His slight hesitation gave them enough time to overcome him. Two of them clutched Max's arms. The third ripped the swim board from his grasp. Max struggled and writhed. He lashed out at the figures, catching one in the face. He heard a muffled grunt of pain – Max was a lot stronger than he had been two months ago – but he couldn't break free. The figure who had taken the swim board disappeared to the west. Only when the thief was out of sight did the other two loosen their grip on Max. Unlike him, they were wearing flippers. They were fast as they followed the first figure. Within seconds, they had disappeared.

Max's instinct was to speed after them. He even twisted his body in that direction. But he stopped himself. Here, under the water, he had no way of navigating. If he followed, he'd be lost.

His mind was clearing, the panic receding. He knew what this was. Not a real attack, but a test. He couldn't tell for sure that the figures had been Hector, Woody and Angel. But since he'd barely seen anyone else in the past two months, he was pretty sure he'd just been attacked by the Watchers.

Train hard, fight easy.

So what should he do?

He couldn't break the surface. If he did, he would fail the exercise, and he was grimly determined not to let that happen. But nor could he swim blindly underwater. He needed help.

There was no current in the lake. If he didn't swim, he wouldn't drift too far. So he stayed still. He felt his body temperature dropping. He moved closer to the surface, guessing it would be warmer there. And he waited.

It took a minute for the next cadet to arrive. The figure appeared through the gloom below him, the swim board glowing faintly. Max plunged down and seized the cadet by the shoulders. The cadet twisted in the water, plainly surprised and perhaps a little scared. Max saw it was Sami. When Sami realised it was only Max, he immediately grew calmer. He inclined his head as if to say: what's up?

They couldn't talk underwater, of course. Max had to mime what had happened. Sami seemed to understand. He pointed at his own swim board, indicating that Max should continue next to him. They were preparing to set off when a third figure appeared: Lili. She cut through the water like a fish but stopped when she saw Max and Sami. She inclined her head, just as Sami had done.

Then the Watchers hit again.

They had the element of surprise and they had superior strength. Lili was expert in four martial arts, but they were no use to her underwater. Three against three, the Watchers tore away Sami and Lili's swim boards in seconds before disappearing.

Lukas arrived. His head was darting left and right. He had no swim board. The Watchers had clearly made their attack, and he was panicking. At first, he appeared relieved to see the others. But when he realised none of them had swim boards he punched the water angrily.

Max noticed something. Nobody had suggested breaking the surface. If the Watchers wanted to play games, that was fine. But there was no way the cadets were going to give in that easily. He pointed back the way they had come. Abby was their last hope. If she lost her swim board, they had no chance of reaching the far end of the lake. The others nodded keenly.

Max led the way back, hoping he was following the right

trajectory. He soon realised he was because he could see the glow of a swim board. And attacking from three directions were the familiar figures of the three Watchers.

Max, Sami, Lili and Lukas cut through the water as fast as they could. They reached Abby just as the largest of the figures – who had to be Hector – was ripping the board from her grasp.

The cadets were like the shoal of fish he had seen earlier: fast and agile. Max and Lili cut silently through the water towards Hector. Max grabbed Abby's swim board. Lili ripped Hector's rebreathing mask from his face. The Watcher was suddenly surrounded by a fierce cloud of bubbles. Max could just see his expression. He could tell Hector was shocked at the suddenness of their attack. But he had water in his rebreathing apparatus. There was little he could do other than escape to the surface. Max spun round. He saw more bubbles. Lukas and Sami had done the same thing to Woody and Angel. Neutralised, they headed to the surface.

Max handed the swim board back to Abby. She gave him a thumbs-up and checked her trajectory on the glowing compass. The others surrounded her: Max and Lili on either side, Sami above her and Lukas just behind. There were no instructions. The cadet team was thinking as a single unit. They moved as one too, slicing through the icy water in a well-ordered group. Max was on high alert for another attack by the Watchers, but he knew deep down that it wouldn't come. Their rebreathing apparatus was out of play. The cadets had the upper hand.

It took, Max estimated, forty-five minutes to reach the far end of the lake. With each stroke, he felt his energy sapping, thanks to the low temperature and the exertion. But the cadets kept their shape and, when the water suddenly became shallow enough for them to stand, they emerged in an arrowhead formation. Water sluiced from their bodies. Each of them was shivering. But they had done it.

Max heard a buzzing. He removed his rebreathing mask and looked back. A speedboat was emerging from the mist that had settled on the lake. He squinted. Hector was at the wheel. Woody and Angel were behind him. Angel's fiery red hair, pulled back in a tight ponytail, almost glowed in the mist. Woody's sandy hair and broken nose normally made him seem oddly friendly, but now his brow was furrowed, his expression serious. The cadets stood, ankle deep, watching the speedboat approach.

'So, er, did we do well?' Sami said.

'We worked as a team,' Lili replied.

'It was the right thing to do,' Sami agreed earnestly.

'I think that's what they wanted us to do,' Abby said.

Lukas scowled. 'I think they just wanted to make our lives more difficult.' Max knew his friend well enough to realise he'd be embarrassed at having lost his swim board.

'Ah well,' Abby said, 'at least we worked up an appetite, hey? By the way, thanks for helping out back there. I could probably have fought them off myself, but you know . . . the more the merrier.'

Max said nothing. The speedboat was close. It swerved round to come to a sideways halt close to the shore, sending a wave almost up to the cadets' knees. The three Watchers were wet and they wore steely expressions. From the back of the boat, Angel caught Max's eye. She gave him a thumbs-up, which meant: you did well.

But there were no congratulations from Hector. 'Will you stop standing around feeling pleased with yourselves,' he bellowed. 'A job's come in. You're being deployed!'

Max blinked. He looked around at his fellow cadets. They were all staring at the speedboat in surprise.

'What are you, stupid?' Hector screamed. '*Get into the boat! Now!*'

2

Eavesdropping

There was no way they could ask what was happening during the journey back across the lake. The motor was too loud and there was spray in their faces. The cadets were shivering, their hands mottled blue.

The lake was situated at the far end of the valley they now thought of as home. Still wearing their diving gear, they bundled into a minibus. It sped over rough ground, past a forested area and a gun range, towards a bleak old stone building. This was Valley House. It was where they ate and slept. It was also where they spent their free time, though there wasn't much of that. The Watchers seemed to have something for them to do every waking moment.

The minibus screeched to a halt in between the house and some iron Nissen huts the cadets had used during selection. They exited the bus and, with frozen limbs, tramped into Valley House. As they moved along the corridor, Max couldn't help glancing at the pictures that lined the wall. One was an old photo showing a young man whose features were almost identical to Max's. He knew now that it was his late father, who had founded the Special Forces Cadets many years ago. Hector had been a friend of Max's father, and blamed himself for his death. That was why he was tougher on Max than on the others. He wanted to ensure that Max truly had the tools to stay alive in their dangerous business.

'Briefing room in twenty minutes,' Hector announced before he, Woody and Angel disappeared up the stairs. The cadets headed towards their ground-floor dormitories: one for Max, Sami and Lukas; one for Abby and Lili. There was a warm boot room adjoining the boys' dormitory, where they stripped out of their clammy wetsuits and took hot showers in their individual cubicles. The walls were plain concrete, the lights flickering strips. There was nothing luxurious about their quarters. It was the cadets' job to keep them clean. None of them dared complain about it to Hector. They knew better than to appear pampered.

Back in the dormitory – where they had a bed, a wardrobe and a bedside table each, nothing more – they pulled on dry clothes. Nobody spoke. They had only been on one operation before this. It had been traumatic and dangerous. Max suspected the others would be as anxious as he was at the thought of being deployed again. They didn't need him to bring it up, so he kept quiet.

Just as he was finishing getting dressed, Abby entered.

'Hey!' Lukas said. He was shy about being seen without his shirt on. Max had noticed that he went out of his way to cover up the gang tattoos on his dark skin.

'Ah, you're so coy, Lukas,' Abby said, winking at him. 'C'mon, you lot. Our room. We can hear them.'

The girls' dormitory was almost identical to the boys', and just as spartan. There were two beds rather than three, and an exposed heating pipe. It ran from the ceiling, down one corner of the room and along the wall. Abby had discovered its strange properties within a week. The pipe led up to the main room on the first floor. It was a large room with tall windows facing out over the valley. It was here that Hector often spoke to Woody and Angel about the cadets' progress. They knew this, because if they put their ears to the pipe and remained still and silent, they could just make out voices in the room above. On occasion Max had wondered if the adults knew they could be overheard. Whenever the cadets had tried to eavesdrop, the conversations had been bland and uninteresting. Occasionally they had learned what training exercise awaited them the following day. Fitness, maybe, or counter-surveillance, or navigation, or one of the other myriad skills they were being taught . . . But apart from that, nothing.

This morning was different. As Max put his ear to the pipe, he heard muffled voices talking over each other. He screwed up his face as he tried to tune his ear into the indistinct sound.

'It's too dangerous,' Angel was saying. 'The three of us can't realistically be nearby. They'll be on their own. And you know what'll happen if they get caught.'

'If you want to argue it out with our superiors, be my guest,' Hector replied.

'Seems to me,' Woody said, 'that the Special Forces Cadets are getting a little too good at digging our superiors out of a hole.'

'Amen to that,' Hector said. A pause. 'This lot are good.

14

Better than I expected. They made short work of us in the lake.'

'You're not going to tell me you're proud of them, Hector?' Angel said.

'He didn't look proud of them when Lili ripped that mask off his face,' Woody chuckled.

'Have you two quite finished? The cadets will be up here any minute. I need to get back on the radio and find out more about the operation. If those kids are being sent into North Korea –'

Max didn't hear the end of Hector's sentence. Lili gasped and pulled away from the pipe. 'What's wrong?' Sami asked, his forehead creased with concern.

'North Korea . . .' Lili whispered. 'It's . . . it's a terrible place.'

'I've heard of it,' Abby said. 'But I don't know much about it. Why's it so bad?'

'It's a dictatorship,' Lili said. 'The government has absolute power over the people, and they have no freedom to do what they want. Wherever they go, there is someone watching them. Whatever they do, it is reported back to the police or the authorities. If they say something bad about the government, they are put in prison. But not an ordinary prison. Hard labour camps, concentration camps. Sometimes they are not sent to prison at all. Sometimes they just disappear. Everybody knows that they are killed, but people are too scared to say anything.'

'How come you know so much about it?' Lukas asked.

'North Korea shares a border with China. It is over eight

hundred miles long. Sometimes defectors cross the border to escape into China and people hear their stories. Most North Koreans would prefer to cross over into South Korea. But that's almost impossible. Anybody seen trying to cross that border would be immediately shot. There are rumours – I don't know if they're true – that the government electrocutes certain rivers that people might use to escape. There are food shortages, electricity shortages . . . there are shortages of everything.'

'Except bullets, by the sound of it,' Max said.

Lili nodded. 'They hold public executions in North Korea, and even children are forced to attend. In the countryside, people are starving. You can see bodies by the road where people have died of hunger. And in the labour camps . . .' She shook her head, as if trying to rid herself of a thought.

'What?' Abby said quietly.

'I read somewhere that when people die in the camps, the bodies are left out for the rats. They eat the eyeballs first, so the corpses look like zombies . . .'

The cadets stared at her in horror. 'They won't be sending us to one of those places, surely?' Sami said in a quiet voice.

'I don't think so,' Lili said uncertainly. 'There are parts of North Korea that are supposed to be safe for tourists.'

'Tourists?' Abby said. 'Who'd want to go there on holiday?'

'Well, I don't really know. Just people who are interested, I suppose. They go to the capital. It's called Pyongyang. But they are accompanied everywhere by a North Korean guide. They are only allowed to see the parts of the city the government wants them to see.'

'I heard that the Americans were trying to improve their relationship with the North Koreans,' Max said. 'Maybe things are better there now?'

'If they're better,' Lukas said darkly, 'why are *we* being sent there?'

Nobody had an answer to that. They sat in silence. It occurred to Max that Valley House was a bleak and uncomfortable place. But all of a sudden it truly felt like home. As an orphan, he'd never had that feeling about anywhere. He realised he didn't want to leave.

'We'd better go,' said Sami. 'They'll be waiting for us.'

The cadets stood up quietly. They filed out of the girls' dormitory and up the stairs to the room where the Watchers waited for them.

Their faces were grim. Max could tell this was going to be serious.

3

Missing

'Okay, listen up,' Hector said before they even had a chance to take a seat on one of the armchairs or sofas dotted around the room. He stood behind a desk, his palms pressed down on the top. Woody and Angel stood by the window. Woody's sandy hair was still damp, his friendly face ruddy from the cold. Angel's fiery red hair, normally pulled back into a tight ponytail, was dishevelled. 'Green Thunder will touch down at the landing zone in about fifteen minutes.'

Green Thunder was the Special Forces Cadets' helicopter. The valley was inaccessible by foot. Green Thunder was used to transport them from this inaccessible location to wherever they needed to be.

Hector raised his hands and cracked his knuckles. 'Right. North Korea. What do you know about it?'

The cadets glanced at Lili.

'Bits and pieces,' Max said.

Hector pretended not to have heard him. 'The Korean Peninsula is situated between China and Japan. It split into north and south after the Second World War. South Korea is a modern, thriving country. North Korea is a brutal police state run by despots. There is no freedom of speech, no freedom of movement. For Western intelligence agents and military personnel, it's one of the most dangerous places on earth. It's no great secret that the West sends spies into North Korea. If they are discovered, they are dealt with brutally.'

'How?' Lukas asked.

Hector glanced over at Woody and Angel, then back at Lukas. 'The last time the North Korean secret police questioned a suspected spy, they deported him back to the USA. He died within days of his return, having suffered severe brain damage. Put it this way: he didn't get that from combing his hair. And the worst thing was that the North Koreans had got it wrong. He wasn't a spy. He was just a student who'd wandered off the beaten path and found himself somewhere he shouldn't have been. He was a tourist, not an intelligence agent.'

Hector let that sink in before continuing.

'There *are* Western spies in North Korea of course. There have to be. For years, North Korea has been developing nuclear weapons. It's something the West really doesn't want. The British, the Americans, the French, the Germans, the Australians: we all want to know what's going on with the North Korean nuclear programme. So we send agents into the country to gather information.' Hector sniffed. 'That's what this is about. One of our people – one of our *best* people – is missing. We believe the authorities have the agent in custody now.'

The cadets stared at him. Were they all remembering, like Max was, what Lili had told them about life in North Korea? He wondered what this captured spy was enduring at this moment.

'The North Koreans are demanding an exchange,' Hector continued. 'The South Koreans have captured two high-level North Korean agents. The North Koreans want to swap their two for our one.'

'Then why not do that?' Lili asked. She sounded relieved that there might be a straightforward solution to the problem.

'It's not that simple.'

'Sounds simple to me,' Lukas said.

'We know how the North Korean secret police operate. Before making any exchange, they will torture our agent. The agent will be able to hold out for maybe seventy-two hours before spilling everything they know. And remember the American tourist I told you about. Our agent may not survive the interrogation process. The exchange the North Koreans are proposing would guarantee nothing: not the safety of our agent, nor the secrecy of any information they have.'

Woody wandered to the middle of the room. He gave the cadets an encouraging smile. 'There's something you need to understand,' he said.

'Make it quick,' Hector told him. 'We don't have much time.'

'We have time for this. It's important. The exercise we did in the lake this morning? Sure, you learned how to use a rebreather. But you've probably worked out that it was about something else. Anyone care to guess?'

There was a moment of silence. Then Lukas said: 'Teamwork?'

'Right.' Woody smiled again. 'It's the most important lesson you'll ever learn in this job. Once you're in the team, we've got your back. If you're in trouble, there's nothing we won't do to get you *out* of trouble. But the team is bigger than you think. It's not just the five of you. It's every agent, every undercover operator and every soldier. If one of our people is compromised, we do whatever it takes to help them. This agent in North Korea is one of us. One of you. And if they're one of us, they don't get left to their fate.'

'Very touching,' Hector muttered.

'I still don't get it,' Max said. 'I thought the whole point of the Special Forces Cadets is that we go into situations that aren't suitable for adults.'

'If you'd let me finish?' Hector said pointedly. 'The North Korean authorities will be *expecting* a rescue attempt. They already have a heightened level of security at all their border crossings. Tourists are being turned away for the flimsiest reasons, just on the off-chance that they might be agents. We *could* parachute in regular Special Forces, but it would take time for them to mobilise and it would be hard for them to operate on the streets of Pyongyang because they'd look so different to regular members of the public. We need people who can cross the border quickly, legally and without suspicion and who have a legitimate reason for being in North Korea. That's where you lot come in.'

'How do we enter legally?' Abby asked. Unlike Max, she was not shouted down.

'There are tour companies who specialise in bringing Westerners into Pyongyang for a few days' sightseeing. The five of you will be registered with one of these companies. Your guides won't know your real identities, which is safer for them. But they are experts in moving tourists in and out of the country. We're confident you'll be allowed in if you're with them.'

'Then what?' Sami asked.

'Then you get to work. British intelligence are well informed about North Korea. They know the location of most of the interrogation facilities. And the North Koreans *know* that they know. As they are plainly expecting a rescue mission, they have ensured that the spy is not being held in any of these facilities.'

'So where is he?' Lili asked.

'Pyongyang is on a river,' Hector said. 'It cuts the city in two. We think our target is locked up on a secure boat moored to a pier on the northern bank of the river.'

'Why a boat?' Abby asked. 'Why not a prison? They're kind of hard to break out of. Trust me.' Max remembered that Abby had been born in a tough Northern Irish prison.

'But they're pretty easy to break in to,' Angel said. 'Trust *me*, hun – I've done it a few times. And there's another reason boats are better than buildings. If you're expecting a rescue attempt, boats can move. Buildings can't.'

'Keeping our agent on this boat in the centre of Pyongyang means that the officials and interrogators in Pyongyang have easy access,' Hector said. 'But the boat can also move downriver to a new location if a rescue attempt is suspected.'

'And let's not skirt around the issue,' Angel said. 'It's easy to dispose of a body quickly in a river.'

'Right,' Hector agreed. He looked around. 'Your mission is this: enter Pyongyang and help the spy escape from the boat before the North Korean authorities have a chance to do their worst.'

'What's his name?' Abby asked. 'The spy, I mean.'

'We can't tell you.'

'Why not?'

Hector exchanged a meaningful glance with Woody and Angel. 'Because our agent has a family,' he said.

'I don't understand –'

'It's obvious, isn't it?' Max interrupted. 'If one of us is caught, and we know the spy's real name, it won't be long before they torture it out of us. And when that happens, the spy's family is at risk.'

A heavy silence fell on the room as the cadets considered that possibility.

'Max is right,' Hector said. 'The less you know about your target, the less you can reveal. For now we will refer to our agent only by a codename: Prospero.'

'There's something else I don't get,' Max said. 'If this boat contains a high-level target, it's going to be well guarded.'

'Right,' said Hector.

'And I'm guessing there will be armed personnel on the pier where it's moored.'

'You bet.'

'So how do we gain access?'

'I'd have thought that would be obvious,' Hector said. 'You swim. Woody's wrong: this morning's exercise wasn't *only* about teamwork.' He cocked his head as if he heard something. Then Max heard it too. The distant throbbing of helicopter rotors.

'That's Green Thunder,' Hector said. 'We need to board. We'll brief you further when you're in transit. Don't just stand there staring at me. Get going. Prospero's life could depend on how fast we move.'

4

First Class

There was no time to make any preparations. The cadets didn't even return to their dormitories. The Watchers hurried them out of Valley House to the landing zone. Green Thunder, a twin-rotor Chinook helicopter, had touched down. Its tailgate was opening. Max felt a surge of something in his gut: half excitement, half terror. The last time they'd left Valley House in Green Thunder, they had almost never returned. But still, the adrenaline rush was there.

Inside the aircraft, he and the others strapped themselves in. The tailgate closed and then they were airborne. They each had a set of headphones fitted to the wall behind their benches. Once they all had them on, the pilot spoke. 'We'll be putting you down on the tarmac at Heathrow in approximately two and a half hours. British Airways is delaying a flight to Beijing for you. It's a full flight. Get ready for some dirty looks from the other passengers.'

Max happened to be watching Lili as the captain spoke. Her face lit up when the captain mentioned China, then she bowed her head. There would be no time for visiting now they were on ops.

Apart from that terse communication, they heard nothing from the flight deck for the remainder of the journey. The cadets sat uncomfortably in the dark, noisy belly of the Chinook. The reek of aviation fuel caught the back of Max's throat. His body vibrated with the hum of the aircraft. It struck him that it had been a very busy morning. 'Better than school,' he muttered to himself. Lukas, sitting opposite, inclined his head questioningly. 'Nothing,' Max mouthed.

They touched down just after midday. An unmarked airport transit bus was waiting for them. As the cadets filed down the tailgate of the Chinook, Max saw a man in military uniform waiting by the bus. He stared at the cadets with open curiosity.

'Eyes forward, soldier,' Hector said.

The soldier saluted and handed Hector a briefcase. Hector took it wordlessly and entered the bus. The cadets followed. As the bus roared across the tarmac, Max looked back. The soldier was staring after them. He wondered what the soldier would tell his mates back in barracks about the five teenagers landing at Heathrow by Chinook.

The bus approached an enormous passenger aircraft, gleaming white in the midday sunshine. Since joining the Special Forces Cadets, Max had made several journeys by helicopter. Before then, he had lived in a residential care home. Holidays had been rare and foreign travel unthought-of. He had never been in an aeroplane, and he felt apprehensive.

'You okay, Max?' Lili asked him quietly as he stared at the plane.

'Fine,' Max said, suddenly embarrassed by his lack of experience.

'Give it a couple of months,' Woody said from behind them, 'and you'll be learning how to jump out of one of these beauties, or something like it. That's when the fun really starts!'

Max did his best to smile. 'Can't wait. Er, I guess we'd better board?'

Hector was urging them out of the transit bus. They walked across the tarmac and up the airstair that led to the front entrance of the aircraft. There was no security, nobody to check if they had passports – which they didn't. An air steward was waiting for them. Max thought he seemed annoyed at having to wait for them. He led them up an internal staircase to the top deck of the aircraft. It was luxurious here. Each passenger had their own cubicle. The cadets and their Watchers received several frowns as they moved up to the front of the cabin, where there was a curtained-off section. Behind the curtain were eight cubicles and a central seating area. It was extremely comfortable. The cadets gazed around in wonder. Max could tell he wasn't the only cadet unaccustomed to these surroundings.

'Is this first class?' Lukas said.

Hector nodded.

'Wicked,' Lukas said. He gave one of his rare smiles.

The Watchers, on the other hand, barely seemed to notice the luxury. 'Don't get used to it,' Hector told them. 'Now buckle up. We'll continue our briefing once we're airborne.'

Max selected one of the cubicles. His body sank into the

comfortable seat. This, he decided, was a lot better than Green Thunder. It was with reluctance, once they were in the air and the 'fasten seatbelts' sign had been extinguished, that he re-joined the others at the seating area. Abby, who seldom talked about anything apart from her next meal, was holding an airline menu. 'We get to order food, right?'

Hector blinked at her. 'What?'

'In case you hadn't noticed, we haven't eaten since last night, and that was Martha's cooking.' She scanned the menu. 'I'm thinking roast beef and sticky toffee pudding.'

'Get it down you, girl,' Angel said. 'The grub will be terrible in Pyongyang.'

'Just sit down, everyone,' Hector said. 'You can eat later. This is more important.'

The cadets took their seats and waited for Hector to continue.

'When we land in Beijing, you will make contact with the travel firm who will take you into Pyongyang. Your guides' names are Jerry and Elsa. They run a company specialising in trips to North Korea. Our information is that they're not the most organised or safety-conscious. Ordinarily, we wouldn't touch them with a barge pole. In this instance, that's what we want, because you'll need to hoodwink them. Accompanied by Jerry and Elsa, you will fly from Beijing to Pyongyang. Arrival time, approximately 07:40 hours local time.'

'How old are Jerry and Elsa?' Sami asked.

'Mid-twenties.'

'Won't they be under suspicion?'

'We don't think so,' Hector said. 'They go in and out of

North Korea so often that they're almost beyond suspicion. The authorities know them well, and they're familiar faces at border security.'

'Won't it seem strange that we don't have any luggage?' Lukas said.

'You'll be supplied with suitcases when we land in Beijing. The suitcases will be specially packed to ensure the officials at Pyongyang airport have nothing to complain about, if and when they examine them. But you'll need to make sure you can recognise them. Once you're through airport security, a British embassy official will make contact. He will have identical cases with very different contents. You will swap your safe suitcases for the new ones. This must happen covertly. If anybody finds out what's in the new suitcases, you're looking at twenty years in a hard labour camp.'

The cadets stared at him. Nobody spoke.

'The suitcases will contain everything you need for the operation. Wetsuits. Rebreathing apparatus. Underwater welding units. A chain cutter. Encrypted satellite phones – these are highly illegal in North Korea. And a weapon.'

'Is the airport really the best place to make the swap?' Max said. 'Won't surveillance be really high?'

'Surveillance is high everywhere in North Korea. Sometimes it's best to do these things in the open.'

'I'll take your word for it,' Abby muttered.

'Do that,' Hector said. 'Hiding in plain sight is a skill you'll need to learn. Almost all foreign visitors to Pyongyang stay in the same hotel. You'll remember I said that the city has a river running through it. The hotel is situated on a small island in the middle of the river. When you make your rescue attempt, you will gain access to the water from the hotel.'

'But people will see us if we just jump in the river,' said Sami.

Hector nodded. 'You will have to do it covertly. The British security services are in possession of detailed construction plans showing the hotel's layout. There is a sewer system leading from the basement out into the river. You will get into the sewer and access the river from there.'

'Get *into* the sewer?' Abby said, wrinkling her nose.

'That's right.'

'You know, suddenly I'm not so hungry after all.'

'It won't be nice,' Hector agreed. 'But it's the safest way. Four of you will access the basement . . .'

'Why only four of us?' Lukas interrupted.

'One of you needs to stay behind in the hotel so you can act if anything goes wrong. I suggest it should be Lili.'

'What?' Lili said. 'Why?'

'Because you can pass as Korean,' Hector said. 'If necessary, you can move around the capital more easily.'

Lili frowned. She didn't have an answer to that.

'You'll need to access the basement via a disused laundry chute on the fifth floor of the hotel,' Hector continued. 'But there's a problem.'

'You don't say,' Abby muttered.

'The fifth floor is out of bounds to guests. It doesn't appear on the lift buttons. You can only access it by stairs. We don't know what else happens on the fifth floor, but we do know you mustn't be caught there. You will abseil down the laundry chute and follow the sewer system into the river. You'll put on your rebreathing apparatus and swim towards the prison barge. Obviously you must do this at night, when you're expected to be in bed and asleep.'

'Obviously,' Lukas said.

'The underwater welding unit is a piece of apparatus that allows you to cut through metal when it's underwater, using a powerful flame. Special Forces use them regularly for underwater operations. You must use this unit to make a hole in the barge's hull. This will scuttle the barge. As it sinks, the guards will only be thinking about saving themselves. This will give Prospero the opportunity to escape. You'll have the chain cutter in case Prospero is chained up inside the boat, and you are to hand over the weapon before going your separate ways. Prospero will know what to do from that point on. You lot are to return to your hotel and carry on with your trip as if nothing has happened. You'll return to the UK two days later.'

The cadets stared at him. Max could guess what they were thinking: that this sounded insanely dangerous. He shivered. Suddenly his first-class surroundings didn't seem so comfortable.

'I'm not going to lie,' Abby said quietly. 'I've always been terrified of drowning. I'm beginning to wish we'd spent more time learning to dive and less time on the old Morse code.'

'Morse is an important skill,' Hector said.

'Sure,' Abby retorted. 'If it's World War Two.'

Max headed off the argument. 'When the North Koreans

realise that Prospero has escaped,' he said, 'surely British tourists like us will be under even tighter surveillance.'

'Probably,' Hector said. 'You might even be deported. But our superiors are calculating that the North Koreans will not risk letting teenage tourists come to harm, not after the business with the student who came back brain damaged. They don't care much about bad publicity, but even they would draw the line there. You're a lot younger than he was, after all.'

'What if it all goes wrong?' Lili asked. 'Is there a plan B?'

'There is,' Hector said. 'You will have two encrypted satellite phones, which mean you will be able to keep in contact with each other and with us. If anything happens to compromise the mission, you must send a distress call. We will mobilise an extraction team to get you out of the country.'

'How?' Lili said.

'Two miles to the south of Pyongyang there is a deserted football stadium. I'll give you the precise location at the end of the briefing. This football stadium fell into disuse years ago. We will have a stealth helicopter on stand-by across the border in South Korea. If you make the distress call, the chopper will risk breaching North Korean airspace to meet you at the rendezvous point. We will extract you from there. But I can't emphasise this enough: it is an emergency measure only. The North Korean government will consider a breach of their airspace to be an act of war. The consequences of that could be disastrous.'

'No pressure then,' Abby said.

'Where will you three be?' Max asked.

'We can't enter the country,' Hector said. 'We would draw too much suspicion. While you're entering Pyongyang, we will travel to the border with South Korea. There's an area of no man's land between the two countries. It's called the demilitarised zone, or DMZ. We'll be stationed just south of the DMZ with the stealth chopper. If you need to call for an extraction, we'll be on the chopper when it comes to get you.'

'Will we have a local chaperone?' Lili asked. 'I've heard that foreigners are required to have a North Korean with them at all times.'

'That's right,' Hector said.

'So how do we shake them off?' Abby said.

'You'll have to work that one out for yourselves,' Hector said. 'We can't plan everything for you.' He looked at them in turn. 'Over the past two months we've been concentrating on your physical fitness. Don't get me wrong – that will be important. The swim from the hotel to the prison barge will be difficult and exhausting. But agents don't succeed on missions like this because of the size of their muscles. They succeed because of their brains. You will have to think quick and think smart. And remember this: the North Koreans are not bad people. They are good people, with a bad government. That government scares, terrorises and brainwashes them. Be careful who you speak to, and what you say. Deception comes easily when you're scared for your life and that of your friends and family. Trust nobody.'

Max stared at the Watchers. Their faces were so grim it gave him a cold feeling in his stomach.

'Let's get some food,' Woody said. But Max could tell that they had all lost their appetite. Even Abby.

5

Sunlight

Beijing airport was busy and crowded, even though it was early. The cadets cleared security on their own. They had said goodbye to their Watchers while still on the plane. Their briefing had continued for most of the flight. Hector, Woody and Angel had covered as many aspects of the operation as they could think of: how to abseil down the laundry chute in the hotel, how to use a state-of-the-art GPS system to navigate in the river without swim boards, which were too bulky to be easily supplied in-country, how to operate the underwater welding unit. They carefully studied the plans of the hotel where they would be staying, and repeatedly went over their strategy for the rescue mission. But no matter how well briefed they were, it was nerve-racking saying goodbye to their Watchers. Angel's parting words hardly helped. 'We'll disembark last,' she said. 'From now on, assume you're under surveillance. From the moment you say goodbye, you're five kids travelling alone.'

Max's body clock was already out of sync. They had left the UK at about midday London time. The flight to Beijing had been ten hours long, but they were seven hours ahead of London time. It meant it was 05:00 hours local time.

The cadets were tired, but they couldn't let that affect them. Their mission was under way.

Hector had issued them each with a valid passport and a further set of instructions. They were to head to the baggage reclaim carousel, where five suitcases would arrive for them. Each suitcase would have two ribbons tied to the handle. Max's would be red and yellow. They would take these suitcases through security in Pyongyang. They contained nothing but clothes and toiletries. Max's case had a hard grey body and was scuffed from much use. It arrived before the others. He stood to one side while his fellow cadets retrieved their own suitcases. They were all different, all well-worn. In his peripheral vision, Max saw Woody enter the baggage reclaim hall. He avoided eye contact. They were operating alone now.

The cadets were silent as they followed the signs – half in Mandarin, half in European languages – to the arrivals hall. Here, it was even busier. There were perhaps thirty or forty cab drivers and tour operators holding up cards with their clients' names on them. Max pinpointed a young man with shoulder-length blond hair and a straggly beard holding up a card that said 'Young Explorers'. The cadets walked up to him. 'Jerry?' Max said.

The young man grinned. 'Hey,' he said. 'Cool! You must be my guys!' He received raised eyebrows from Abby and Lili. 'And girls,' he said.

'Young women,' Abby corrected him.

'Right . . . cool!' He had a slow, lazy voice, as if he had just got out of bed. 'Let's go find Elsa. She's just this way.'

The cadets followed him through the crowds, wheeling

their suitcases behind them. They found Elsa standing by a map of the terminal. She had dreadlocked hair, tied back in a ponytail, a nose stud and the same friendly grin as Jerry. 'No adults!' she said. 'Awesome! Look, you guys . . .'

'. . . and young women,' Jerry interrupted.

'Right! You're probably pretty tired after your long flight. But our connecting flight to Pyongyang leaves in an hour and security can be pretty tight round here. We'd better get moving. This is all kinda last-minute, huh? Your school called and booked us last night.'

'Right,' Max said. 'We were going to go with another company, but they pulled out. I think one of them fell ill? We've been really looking forward to the trip.'

That seemed to satisfy their two guides. They led them across the arrivals hall to a check-in desk. There was no queue here. Flights to Pyongyang were plainly not popular. Maybe it was because it was so early. Maybe it was something else. Their passports were carefully scrutinised and boarding passes provided. They followed Jerry and Elsa to a gate at the far end of the terminal. A small aircraft was already waiting there. It had propellers on the wings and looked old. 'We're really going to get into that thing?' Abby asked under her breath.

'We really are,' Max said.

There were about thirty other passengers. They were mostly Chinese or North Korean, although there were a handful of Westerners. Nobody paid the cadets any attention. Max preferred it that way.

They boarded after twenty minutes. A Western tourist, a couple of places ahead of Max in the queue, tried to take a picture of the plane's interior with his iPhone. One of the air stewardesses welcoming them on board held up a hand. 'No photographs,' she said, looking anxious, as though there could be severe consequences. But she smiled again when the tourist lowered his phone.

The plane was a lot less comfortable than the one from London. The seats were hard and cramped. The aisle carpet had holes in it. When the captain spoke it was in Mandarin, and Max didn't understand a word. He suddenly felt a very long way from home. Sami was on his right, Abby on his left. He wondered if they felt the same.

The take-off was turbulent, but that was nothing compared to the flight itself. The aircraft shook and yawed. They seemed to be in constant cloud and the aircraft's engine sounded like it was struggling. They were presented with plates of unfamiliar food. Abby ate it all hungrily, then finished off what Max and Sami didn't want. Otherwise they sat in silence. It was a long two hours before Max felt the aircraft gradually losing altitude. As the plane banked to the right, he was momentarily blinded by the fiercely bright morning sun. When he regained his sight, he saw a flat landscape stretching off into the distance, with mountains on the horizon. The fields were green, but there did not seem to be much evidence of crops growing. And he could see no big cities, just little pockets of bleak high-rise towers, and roads that, even from this height, appeared to be in need of repair. He felt his nerves biting. All he could think of was swapping over their suitcases at the airport. It made his palms sweat. He wished he could talk to the others about it, but that was impossible. Hector's warning rang in his ears: *trust nobody*. That included Jerry and Elsa. And of course it included their fellow passengers.

07:40 hours local time. Touchdown. The aircraft screeched noisily as it came to a halt. As it taxied off the runway, Max caught sight of the airport terminal through the window. It was not a large building, but was surprisingly modern. It shone in the bright morning sun. Max had expected something much more run-down. Maybe, he told himself, the North Korean authorities wanted to put on a good face to the rest of the world.

Inside the terminal, they queued in single file to show their passports. Max instantly sensed that all was not as it seemed. Unexpectedly cheerful music was playing through the public address system, but the North Koreans he could see did not look cheerful at all. Airport workers stared straight ahead, as if unwilling to catch the eye of any tourists. Security was high. An unsmiling border guard sat in a glass cubicle, flanked by armed soldiers. The guard examined each passport thoroughly for at least two minutes.

'They're not in a rush,' Lukas murmured. He was just behind Max.

'It's like they're making a point,' he agreed.

'What's happening?' Lukas said suddenly.

At the front of the queue the passport control guy was holding the passport of a man in his forties and talking into a phone. Two more armed guards emerged from a room to the right of the cubicle. Wordlessly, they took the man's arms and led him back through the door. There was a nervous murmur along the queue. The next person in line – a woman in her fifties – approached the passport control guy timidly.

When Max's turn finally arrived, he felt himself sweating. Two more people, a man and a woman, had been taken into the other room and had not reappeared. The unsmiling border guard took Max's passport and examined every page in detail. He checked the photo against Max's features several times. His face became more suspicious.

He glanced at his telephone.

Max held his breath. He tried to seem unconcerned but his heart was thumping.

There was no word of welcome. The official simply stamped Max's passport with obvious reluctance and allowed him through. Max had to force himself not to collapse in a relieved heap. He waited for the others. When they arrived, Jerry and Elsa were smiling and as relaxed as ever. Lukas, Sami, Abby and Lili looked as anxious as Max felt. None of them spoke.

As they walked to the baggage reclaim hall, Max had the unpleasant sensation of being watched. He glanced across the hall and locked gazes with an airport official, who looked away immediately. By the carousel, a security guard seemed to be staring at him. He too turned away when Max caught his glare.

The cadets had been waiting for ten minutes before the first suitcase – Lukas's – appeared. The sight of it made

Max shiver involuntarily. Lukas hauled his suitcase from the carousel. The remaining cases arrived within a minute of each other. Having collected them, the cadets congregated a little way from the carousel. Jerry and Elsa joined them. 'What's wrong with you lot?' Jerry smiled. 'You look like you've seen a ghost!'

'They're just a bit nervous, man,' said Elsa. 'Come on. This way. With a bit of luck they won't want to check our cases. There's a car park out the front where we'll meet our chaperone.'

Their luck did not hold. As they wheeled their cases away from the baggage reclaim area, an official called out to Max. Max didn't understand what he said, but his meaning was clear. 'Just do what he wants,' Jerry told him. Max lifted his suitcase on to a table where the official stood. Jerry, Elsa and his fellow cadets had no option but to carry on into the arrivals area, leaving Max on his own.

The official had small round glasses, perched halfway down his nose. He had watery eyes and a jowly face. He seemed suspicious and threatening. He said something in Korean. Max understood it to be an instruction to open up the suitcase. It was all he could do to stop his hands trembling as he unzipped it while the official stared at him over his glasses. Max hadn't packed his case. He had no idea what was in it. Terrible possibilities crowded in his brain. What if someone had got it wrong? What if this suitcase was filled with diving gear, or even contained a weapon? He noticed a camera on the wall behind the official. He was in full view of it, and was certain he was being filmed. He tried not to let his worries show on his face as he opened it up.

The suitcase was filled with clothes and a small wash bag. The clothes were un-ironed and poorly packed – like a young person had done it, not an adult. They didn't smell too fresh. The official peered myopically into the case, rooting around among the clothes unenthusiastically for perhaps ten seconds. He uncovered a pair of aviator-style sunglasses with reflective lenses. Max feigned an expression that said: there they are! He took them from the suitcase and hung them from his shirt. This seemed to offend the guard somehow. Maybe it was because his own eyesight was clearly weak. But he had nothing concrete to complain about. He nodded at Max to indicate that he could close the suitcase and move off. He was already searching for another victim.

The others were waiting for Max out in the arrivals hall. The airport still looked modern. There was a coffee shop, a news stand, a duty-free shop and a couple of restaurants. But somehow, it didn't seem real. Max felt as if they were standing on a temporary film set. There was nobody in the duty-free shop. Nobody queueing for a coffee.

'All set?' Jerry asked.

Max nodded.

'Let's go then.'

The cadets followed their tour leaders towards the exit. The morning sun flooded in through the windows, making Max squint. Lili drew up alongside him. 'When do we swap the suitcases?' she whispered. There were beads of sweat on her forehead.

But Max didn't have an answer. Hector had told them that the British Embassy official would make contact. Well, if that was his plan, Max thought, he'd better do it quickly.

'Oh, excuse me . . .'

A man had walked almost directly into Max. He wore an open-necked shirt and an orange jumper. His chin and cheeks were red with shaving rash. Max, because he was on edge, felt a moment of irritation with the man, who dusted himself down and apologised again. 'Very clumsy of me . . . wasn't really paying attention . . .' He smiled at Max. When he spoke again, he barely moved his mouth. 'Get the bags on to a trolley,' he said quietly. As he spoke, he looked meaningfully across the concourse. Max followed his line of sight. Immediately he saw a young North Korean man with black hair standing just to the right of the coffee shop. He had a luggage trolley. It carried five suitcases. They were identical to the cadets'.

The bumbling man who had bumped into them wandered off. Max, thinking quickly, called ahead to Jerry and Elsa. 'Er, guys?'

'And ladies,' Elsa said archly.

'Right. Er, do you mind if we use the toilet before we go?' He gave a rueful smile. 'Didn't really want to use the one on the plane.'

'Don't blame you, man,' Jerry said, nodding his agreement.

Max affected a nonchalant air. 'So, you go and find our chaperone if you want. We'll meet you outside.'

Jerry and Elsa looked unsure.

'It's fine,' Max assured them. 'Gets us out of this place

quicker.' He waved one arm to indicate the airport.

'Sure, man,' Jerry said. 'We'll be out front.' He and Elsa wandered towards the exit with their suitcases.

Lukas exhaled heavily. 'Those two,' he said. 'They're so laid back they're horizontal.'

'It suits us,' Max said. 'Come with me.' He had noticed a line of luggage trolleys away to their left. The others followed him towards it. Max took a trolley and loaded the five suitcases on to it. The guy with the new suitcases was heading across the concourse towards them. Distance, thirty metres. The others had seen him. Wordlessly, they stepped away from Max, because they were more noticeable as a crowd than as individuals. Max stayed still. Here, by the line of luggage trolleys, he was less exposed. This was the best place to make the swap.

The man with the suitcases was twenty metres away when Max suddenly changed his plan. He had good reason. The official with the little round glasses who had checked his case was walking across the concourse towards them. He was coming from a different angle, but was the same distance away as the suitcase guy. The official's face was hard and suspicious. Max felt a twist of fear in his gut. If this guy noticed the identical suitcases, he would surely want to investigate. And if he searched the right one, he'd find more than a pair of aviator shades.

Aviator shades. They gave Max an idea.

Instinct took over. He swung the trolley round and headed to the exit. In his peripheral vision he saw the suitcase guy look confused. What was Max doing? The guy altered his trajectory and headed towards the exit. Max could sense him over his right shoulder. Spread out, the other cadets followed to his left. Did they know what his plan was? Could they guess?

The exit doors were made of glass. As Max approached he saw the guy with little round glasses behind him, perhaps fifteen metres away. The other cadets had positioned themselves in a group between Max and the official. Good. They knew what he had in mind.

The suitcase guy was approaching an exit to Max's right. Both doors slid open at the same time. As Max pushed the trolley outside, he put on the aviators. He was aware of the suitcase guy putting one hand over his forehead to shield his eyes from the sun. Max scanned the car parking area in front of the terminal. He could see Jerry and Elsa straight ahead. They were standing by a run-down white minibus with a thin North Korean man, perhaps in his early twenties. The minibus was open. Their tour guides were engrossed in conversation, paying no attention to Max.

The suitcase guy drew up alongside Max, who quickly looked over his shoulder. The official had stepped outside. The sunlight had momentarily blinded him. He had removed his round glasses and covered his eyes with one hand.

'Now,' Max whispered.

Instantly, he and the suitcase guy swapped places. The suitcase guy veered off to the left. Max upped his pace and headed straight for the minibus. He looked over his shoulder again. Lukas, Sami, Abby and Lili were in a group just in front of the official, who was putting his glasses on and blinking. The guy with the shaving rash appeared through the exit and spoke to the official. By now, Max was at the minibus. Jerry began to introduce him to the young Korean man, but Max interrupted. 'Shall we get loaded up?'

He started to haul one of the suitcases into the bus. It was very heavy. Jerry took another. 'What you got in here?' he said. 'A body?'

Max smiled nervously and continued loading up. By the time the other cadets arrived, there was only one suitcase left, which he stacked on top of the rest. The British guy was still talking to the official, but didn't have his full attention. He was peering suspiciously towards the minibus.

'Let's go!' Max said. He and the other cadets bundled into the back of the minibus. Jerry and Elsa climbed into the two front passenger seats while the young Korean man took the wheel. Max slid the door shut and the minibus moved off. Through the window he could see the official. He had shaken off the British guy and was squinting after the minibus, then looking in the direction of the suitcase guy. Max, whose heart was thumping fast, could tell the official knew something had happened right under his nose. He just didn't know what.

6

Songbun

Max removed his aviator shades and glanced at the other cadets. They were sitting in two lines down either side of the minibus, with the suitcases piled between them. From the expressions on their faces, and the way none of them looked at the suitcases, Max could guess that the others felt the same mixture of anxiety and relief as he did.

'Guys!' Jerry said from the front, looking over his shoulder to talk to them. 'Meet Hwan. He's going to be our guide while we're here. There aren't many people in NK who speak English. Hwan's the exception.'

The driver held up his right hand. The cadets could only see the back of his head, but Max caught sight of his face in the rear-view mirror. He was unnaturally thin, with a mop of floppy black hair and a narrow, aquiline nose. He smiled. It was a friendly, sad expression. 'Welcome,' he said, 'to my country.' His voice was hushed, but his English was obviously very good.

'How you doing?' Lukas said.

Hwan's face twitched. 'American?' he asked.

'Yeah,' Lukas said.

Hwan kept his eyes on the road.

'What you have to understand,' Elsa said, 'is that from the day they're born, North Koreans are taught that America is the enemy. Hwan here seems pretty enlightened. But I wouldn't go around announcing where you're from to just anybody.'

'Roger that,' Lukas said. The military phrase made Elsa raise an eyebrow. 'I mean, whatever . . .' Lukas mumbled.

They had left the airport complex. Max was relieved to be out of sight of the official with the little round glasses. They found themselves on a main road. The cars travelling in either direction were old and battered, and the road was pot-holed. Beyond the road was flat farmland. In the distance, he could see an ox pulling a plough. The animal was surrounded by a few workers. Max felt he had been dropped back in a different century. The land was dotted with abandoned buildings.

As Lukas spoke, they approached a huge roadside placard. It showed a painting of a smiling Korean man with gleaming teeth and perfectly brushed hair, his head surrounded by a glowing halo. 'Who's that?' Sami asked.

Hwan answered. 'That is the Supreme Leader, Kim Il-sung,' he said. 'We mourn him greatly.' Hwan's voice had a strange, monotone quality. He sounded like he was reciting words he knew by heart.

'Kim Il-sung was the grandfather of the current Supreme Leader, Kim Jong-un,' Jerry said. 'You'll see a lot of pictures of them both, as well as Kim Jong-un's father Kim Jong-il.' He glanced at Hwan. 'Don't, er . . . don't take the mickey,' he said quietly. 'If you fail to be respectful it can get you into a whole heap of trouble.'

Max saw Hwan clenching his jaw. It was almost as if he was nervous about hearing the cadets say something bad about the regime. But they kept silent and he seemed to relax again. Max looked out of the window. The surroundings were becoming more urban. There were concrete tower blocks in the distance, and cranes on the horizon. Closer by, there were little groups of men in orange jackets, sweeping the roadside with old-fashioned brooms. The traffic was not heavy, but there were many people on bicycles. And there were more posters – tens, hundreds of them – portraying the painted features of the supreme leaders. There were pictures of happy, smiling workers in the fields too, and colourful pictures of soldiers in military helmets thrusting assault rifles into the air. One of the largest posters was on top of a concrete tower. It showed a missile marked with an American flag being crushed from above by several enormous fists. Everywhere Max looked there was grey concrete and colourful propaganda posters.

The further they drove into the city, the more people there were. 'Have you noticed that nobody's wearing jeans,' Abby said.

'Jeans are not allowed,' Elsa said. 'Western fashions are frowned upon. Piercings particularly.'

Abby touched her cartilage piercings a little anxiously. She had removed the studs, but the holes were still visible. Max tried to pick out individual faces in the crowd. He had the impression that pedestrians were trying to avoid each other as they passed. 'Why is nobody talking to each other?' he asked.

At first Jerry seemed reluctant to answer. But Hwan showed no emotion.

'They live in fear,' Jerry said in a low voice. He spoke fast to make it hard for Hwan to understand him. 'This is a police state. The government operates a huge system of informants. It's not safe to have risky conversations with anyone, even if they seem friendly. You *never* criticise the government, or the police, or the country. You can't really trust anybody.'

'Do they have, like, phones?' Abby asked. 'Internet? Snapchat?'

'Snapchat, definitely not,' Jerry said with a smile. 'Smartphones are becoming a little more popular, but they can cost half a year's salary so not everybody can have one. There's an internet of sorts, but it's very limited. The people can only access websites that the government permits.'

'So I'm guessing we're not going to kick back and watch some Netflix while we're here,' Abby said.

'Right,' Jerry said. 'No Netflix.'

'Do they have, like, bands . . . celebrities . . . What do teenagers do for fun round here?'

'There are bands, but they're strictly controlled by the regime and they mostly sing propaganda songs.'

'Sounds great . . . not.'

'You can't even buy a radio without permission from the government,' Jerry said, 'and they're specially modified to jam foreign radio broadcasts.' He raised his voice again. 'Hwan's agreed to show us some of the sights before we go to your hotel,' he said.

The cadets glanced at each other, then at the suitcases. Max reckoned they were all thinking the same as him: that they wanted to get the cases stashed away.

'We were hoping to freshen up,' Abby said. 'It's been a long journey.'

'Sights first,' Hwan said. 'Hotel later. That is the itinerary.'

It was clear that there would be no argument.

Pyongyang was not the city Max had expected it to be. Lili's talk of prison camps and bodies left out for the rats had led him to believe that the city would be run-down, dirty and impoverished. It did not seem that way. There were skyscrapers everywhere. They were concrete, not glass, but still imposing. There were wide boulevards and green spaces. There were restaurants and department stores. There were colourful murals alongside the propaganda posters that appeared on almost every street.

And yet, Max could tell Pyongyang was not quite the modern city it pretended to be. There were very few cars on the road. The department stores and restaurants were almost deserted. The open spaces seemed a little too well tended amid the concrete jungle of the tower blocks. There was not a single item of litter on the streets. No graffiti. The crowd of schoolchildren standing in front of a vast stone monument depicting three fists holding tools in the air? They were just a little bit too well-behaved. It was like a show town.

The cadets watched in tense silence as the minibus drove into the centre of Pyongyang. Part of Max's brain was instinctively navigating: the sun was rising to their left, which meant they were heading south. They crossed over a broad waterway.

'The Pothong River,' Hwan announced. These were the first words he had spoken since insisting on giving them a tour of the city.

'It meets the Taedong River further to the south,' Elsa added. 'And your hotel is on a little island on the Taedong River.'

But they didn't head south. Hwan turned left up a long, broad avenue towards an enormous stone arch. Max had never been to Paris, but he had seen pictures of the Arc de Triomphe. This was similar, but larger. Hwan stopped the minibus nearby and urged the cadets to step outside and approach the arch. They did this reluctantly. None of them wanted to leave the suitcases. But to insist on staying in the vehicle would be suspicious. They followed him and listened as he recited a history of the arch, which he plainly knew by heart. 'It was built where our Supreme Leader Kim Il-sung was met with great applause when he returned from victory over the Japanese . . .'

Max stopped listening. He was aware of a middle-aged Korean man standing by the arch, watching them intently. *The government operates a huge system of informants*, Jerry had said. Was this one of them? Or was Max being too suspicious? He'd only been in the country for a couple of hours. Already the place was getting to him.

It was a relief to be back in the minibus, and to see that the suitcases were still there. Untouched. Hwan drove around the Arch of Triumph a couple of times, then headed south along another impressive street. Turning left, the minibus crossed a bridge over a much wider river. 'Oknyu Bridge,' Hwan announced.

'This is the Taedong River,' Jerry said. 'That's your hotel.' He pointed out of the minibus at a tall building set on a little island in the middle of the river. There was a bridge between them and the hotel. The building only commanded Max's attention for a couple of seconds. Instead he found himself examining the banks of the river.

He saw it immediately. Halfway between the two bridges, a pier protruded into the river from the bank. Moored at the end of it was a barge, half a football pitch in length. There were armed guards stationed on the pier and a cordon around the bank. There were three other boats in the vicinity. They were unmarked, but Max was certain they were keeping surveillance on the barge.

The other cadets were staring at it too. Lukas was looking from the hotel to the barge, as if estimating the distance. It was a good hundred and fifty metres, maybe more. A long way to swim.

Max caught Jerry watching him. He immediately stared out of the opposite window. On the other side of the bridge, more boats were moored by the bank. They were small, old and ramshackle. He wasn't sure, but he thought a couple might have outboard motors. But there was no way of accessing these boats, because the river bank was high. You could only get at them from the water.

They cleared the bridge, turned right and approached an enormous obelisk. It was the second sight on Hwan's itinerary and, as they stood underneath it, he recited his pre-learned description in the same monotone. 'This is the Tower of the Juche Ideology. It is the tallest monument in North Korea and is constructed of 25,500 granite blocks. Each block represents a day in the life of the Supreme Leader Kim Il-sung on his seventieth birthday . . .'

But Max wasn't interested in the granite blocks. He was staring across the river at the barge, and thinking about the job they had to do that evening.

The third monument on Hwan's itinerary was back on the other side of Oknyu Bridge. 'The Mansudae Grand Monument,' Hwan explained as they stood in front of it. It comprised two enormous bronze statues. Two groups of schoolchildren were laying flowers at the statues' feet.

'Let me guess,' Abby said, pointing at one of them. 'The Supreme Leader Kim Il-sung.' She put herself in a similar pose, mimicking one of the enormous statues.

'Do not do that . . .' Hwan hissed. 'Please, do not do that.'

He seemed so alarmed that Abby immediately relaxed out of the pose. 'It is not allowed to mimic the Supreme Leader,' Hwan said. All of a sudden he was sweating. 'The punishment is . . . severe.'

'Right,' Abby said, chastened. 'Sorry.'

Hwan continued with his tour-guide monologue. 'These are statues of the Supreme Leaders Kim Il-sung and Kim Jong-il. It is the most sacred monument in North Korea and . . .'

He faltered. Somewhere behind Max, something had caught his attention. Max turned and saw two uniformed police officers approaching. Unsmiling and severe, they wore caps, white jackets and blue trousers. They walked up to Hwan and started to talk to him in Korean, pointing now and then at Abby. They sounded aggressive. Hwan wrung his hands. He inclined his head, bowed and spoke in a calm, humble voice. The cadets couldn't understand him, of course, but it was clear he was digging Abby out of a whole world of trouble. It took at least a minute for the police officers to step back. They narrowed their eyes at Abby, gave Hwan a final curt instruction and moved away. Hwan turned to the cadets. 'We must go,' he said quietly. He was sweating badly and he kept glancing at the two policeman. He met no resistance from the cadets. They were ready to get out of there.

'Thank you,' Abby said as they made their way back to the minibus. 'I'm sorry, I didn't mean . . .'

'You didn't know,' Hwan said. 'It is okay. But do not do it again. Please, for your own safety, do not bring attention to yourself.'

The reprimand from the police officers seemed to have changed Hwan. Before, he had been friendly but a little distant. Now he was obviously scared. Max was warming to him. 'Where do you live?' he asked. 'In Pyongyang?'

Hwan shook his head. He glanced nervously over at the retreating police officers, then spoke quietly so he couldn't be overheard by them. 'Very few people are allowed to live in the city,' he said. 'We call it *songbun*. Only people whose ancestors were of a certain status are allowed to live in the city, have certain jobs, or even . . .' He glanced over at the police again. 'Or even have enough food to eat.'

Max stared at him. 'So where do you live?' he asked quietly.

'Outside Pyongyang, in a village. It is not much. I am the wrong *songbun*.'

'Do your family live with you?' Sami asked.

'No. No family.'

'What about your mum and dad?' Abby asked.

'Please,' Hwan whispered, 'do not keep asking questions. It is not a good idea. Sometimes you don't want to know the answer. Just . . . just complete your tour and leave the country. That is the best thing for you to do.' He lowered his voice even further. 'It is what I would do if I could.'

The cadets knew Hwan had said more than he should have.

'Thank you for helping us back there,' Max repeated. 'We owe you.'

Hwan nodded and they walked back to the minibus in silence. When they were inside, Jerry checked the time. 'It's gone three o'clock,' he said. 'You lot must be tired. I think we should get to the hotel.'

Nobody had any argument. Hwan started the engine and headed back towards the river.

7

Superglue

Yanggakdo International Hotel was one of the tallest buildings in North Korea. Hwan told them this as they walked up to the skyscraper at the eastern end of the small island in the river. He no longer sounded like a tour guide. Some of his stiffness had gone. But he looked nervously around, as if he was checking nobody was watching them.

The cadets wheeled their suitcases into the reception area of the hotel. Max was glad to get inside. The weather had changed. A smog had descended over the city, and although it was still quite cool, it was unpleasant to be outside.

They were in a large reception area with a stone floor and fake pot plants dotted around. There seemed to be too many hotel staff for the number of guests. Apart from the cadets, he could only see three other tourists but counted at least fifteen reception staff. How many were there to greet the guests, he wondered, and how many to spy on them? Certainly the cadets had attracted attention. At least four members of staff were watching them closely.

Hwan, Jerry and Elsa approached the reception desk with the cadets' passports. Check-in took a long time. Twenty minutes at least. There was a lot of paperwork. The cadets themselves stood apart. At first they were silent. After a couple of minutes, they seemed to realise their silence was unnatural and would draw attention to them, so they forced themselves into conversation.

'I wonder what the food will be like,' said Abby.

'That's all you ever think about,' Lukas said.

'No,' Abby replied sweetly. 'Sometimes I think about punching you in the face.'

'It will be quite bland,' said Lili. 'Food is scarce in North Korea, sometimes even for visitors.'

'We must eat as much as we can,' Sami said. He was right. The cold river water would sap their energy. They needed all the fuel they could get, and they'd already skipped lunch. But somehow Max didn't feel hungry.

'I'm glad Hwan managed to talk those two policemen round,' Max said. 'I wasn't sure about him at first, but I think he's a good guy.'

'He didn't want to talk about his family,' said Lili. A concerned expression crossed her face. 'Do you think they're okay? Do you think they're even alive?'

'Who knows?' Lukas said. 'It doesn't matter either way. Remember what Hector said. Trust nobody. That includes Hwan.'

The cadets nodded grimly.

When Hwan, Jerry and Elsa returned, they no longer had the passports but were carrying heavy old-fashioned keys. Two members of the hotel staff accompanied them. 'We're on different floors,' Jerry said. 'Hwan, Elsa and I are on the thirteenth.' He handed out keys. 'Hwan, you're room 1313 – unlucky for some.'

Hwan didn't seem to understand Jerry's comment.

'I'm 1314, Elsa, 1315.' He handed out keys to the cadets. 'And you five are on the ninth, rooms 903 to 908.'

Max glanced at the other cadets. None of them appeared surprised, but he wondered if they were thinking the same as he was. It was convenient that they were on a different floor to the adults. He wondered if the same people who had arranged for the suitcases to be waiting for them at the airport had influence in the hotel too. He guessed he'd never know.

'We're done for sightseeing today,' Elsa said. 'You shouldn't leave the hotel by yourselves. The authorities don't want you talking to civilians. There's a revolving restaurant on the top floor. Let's meet there for dinner at seven, and we'll have a full day of it tomorrow. Sound good?'

The cadets nodded and followed the two hotel staff to the lift on the far side of the reception area. 'Often the lifts in Pyongyang do not work,' Hwan said. But today was not one of those days. They crowded into the lift with their suitcases. Max examined the buttons. They had been warned that the fifth floor would not appear. Sure enough, the sixth-floor button was immediately above the fourth floor. The lift itself made a loud, mechanical creak as it rose to the ninth floor. It opened on to an empty, stale-smelling corridor with a threadbare red carpet and brown walls. The cadets exited the lift, confirmed they would meet Hwan, Jerry and Elsa at seven in the restaurant, and watched the lift shut.

It felt to Max like they all exhaled with relief at the same time.

'Is anyone else freaked out by this place?' Abby said quietly. 'I feel like I'm being watched everywhere I go.'

'Try being black,' Lukas muttered. 'It's like they've never seen someone with dark skin before . . .'

Lili was looking suspiciously up and down the corridor. 'What is it?' Max asked.

'We shouldn't speak too freely,' she said. 'It's probably safe in the corridors, but we can't be sure there aren't listening devices in our rooms.'

'You think the hotel knows about us?' Sami said, clearly anxious.

'No. But surveillance is normal here. We must be careful what we say.'

Their rooms were at the far end of the corridor, just past a water-cooler machine that didn't work. Max's was room 903. He unlocked it and stepped inside. The room was plain and tatty. A double bed, a desk, a chair and a wardrobe. A sink in one corner. No bathroom. Two pictures of the country's smiling leaders on one wall. The ceiling was constructed of panels that looked like they could be removed. The curtains were closed. He switched on the light – it was dim and flickering – and locked the door from the inside. Then he lodged the chair under the handle. He hauled his heavy suitcase on to his bed and opened it, his hands shaking.

He was expecting the contents, but the sight of them still made his heart beat a little faster. His rebreathing apparatus and a wetsuit were tightly packed in a black dive bag. It resembled a plain rucksack, but bulky. There was a second black bag containing one of two underwater welding units – Max knew that the second would be in Abby's case – the chain cutters and a black semi-automatic pistol. The main GPS unit would be with Lukas, the satellite phone with Sami and the high-powered optics with Lili. Thinking about what would have happened if the official at the airport had found any of that stuff made him shudder. He quickly lifted the gear out of the suitcase and stashed it under the bed. There were also a few clothes, toiletries and a spare pair of trainers in the case. Tucked among the clothes there was a small tube of Superglue. He allowed himself a smile. He knew what that was for: the Watchers had taught him how to use Superglue in his first ever counter-surveillance lesson. He put it in his pocket then placed the clothes in the wardrobe before walking over to the window and opening the curtains.

His room faced out on to the river and over Pyongyang. The smog that had increased throughout the day was thicker here. It cast a haze over the Tower of the Juche Ideology and the sea of concrete tower blocks. His gaze was drawn to the river and the pier emerging from its western bank. The prison barge was still there. He counted four patrol boats. They weren't moving, and one was positioned directly between the hotel and the barge. If it was still there tonight, they would have to swim around it.

Max was suddenly overcome with tiredness. He lay on his bed. In seconds, he was asleep.

A knock woke him with a start. He sat up quickly, momentarily unsure of where he was. It was almost dark outside. From his bed he could see lights along the river. The person in the corridor tried the door handle. It jammed against the chair.

'Who is it?' Max called groggily.

There was no answer. The handle noise stopped. Max hauled himself off his bed, removed the chair and opened up. Nobody. He stepped outside and looked along the corridor just in time to see a figure disappearing round the far corner. He had no idea who it was. Just a member of the hotel staff? Or was somebody trying to keep tabs on them?

Sami appeared from the room next to him. 'Are you okay?' he asked.

'Yeah,' Max said, his voice distracted. 'Hey Sami, did someone just knock on your door?'

Sami shook his head. 'You?'

'Yeah.' Max narrowed his eyes. 'Get the others,' he said quietly. 'Tell them to meet in my room.'

'Is everything okay?' Sami said.

Max mouthed the answer silently. 'We're being watched,' he said.

He returned to his room and removed the rebreather apparatus, welding unit and gun from under his bed. He had decided that wasn't a good enough hiding place. He jumped up on to the bed and lifted one of the ceiling panels, revealing an access hole to a cavity above.

The door opened. Max jumped, but it was only the others, who filed in silently. They looked askance at Max, who lifted up his illicit gear, stashed it into the cavity above the bed and replaced the panel. He climbed down from the bed and collected up a few crumbs of plaster that had fallen from the ceiling, which he washed down the sink. Then he pulled the Superglue from his pocket and held it up for the others to see. Nobody said anything, but they nodded in understanding and silently left the room.

Max plucked a hair from his head. He opened the tube of Superglue and applied a tiny amount at either end of the hair. He stood up on the bed again and stuck the hair at the edge of the panel. It was too fine to be visible unless you were searching for it. But if anybody opened the panel while he was having dinner, he'd see that the hair had been dislodged. What then? He guessed they would have no option but to abort the mission. He stepped out of the room and locked it behind him. Then he repeated the process with a second hair, sticking one end to the bottom of the door and the other to the frame. Now he would know if anybody had entered his room.

Lukas appeared next. He nodded at Max and, using his own tube of Superglue, stuck a hair at the bottom of his door. Sami, Abby and Lili exited and did the same. None of them had spoken a word to each other.

'Dinner?' Abby said.

'Dinner,' the others replied in unison.

They took the lift to the top-floor restaurant. It was circular, but revolved so slowly that you could barely notice it. It was almost fully dark outside and they had a good view over Pyongyang. Max noticed that only certain sectors of the city were lit up. Could whole areas be disconnected from the power supply? But there was one light that grabbed his attention. It was a single moving floodlight on the southern bank of the river. It was scanning the water surrounding the prison barge. Max was reminded of prison camp spotlights in old war movies. He suppressed a shudder at the thought of what would happen if it illuminated one of them in the water later that night . . .

Hwan was sitting with Jerry and Elsa. He had his head bowed over his food and was eating intently. Max remembered what Lili had said about food being scarce in North Korea. The cadets approached a serving area at one end of the restaurant. Max recognised nothing on the hotplates. An unsmiling young man handed him a plate of food. He and the other cadets took their plates to the table and sat with the others.

Hwan had finished his food. Jerry and Elsa were picking over theirs unenthusiastically. Their North Korean guide couldn't help staring at the others' dinner. Max had the impression that he was still hungry. He tried a few mouthfuls. There were cold noodles, somewhat congealed, and a piece of something raw and rubbery. Octopus, maybe? It wasn't to his taste and he found he wasn't hungry anyway. It was probably nerves. He found himself thinking about what Hwan had said regarding *songbun*. 'I don't think I want this,' he told Hwan. 'You can have it, if you like.'

Sami gave him a look that said: you need to eat. Max ignored it. Hwan seemed a little embarrassed, but he accepted the food with a silent bow and ate it slowly, as if savouring every mouthful.

Jerry and Elsa gave them a run-down of the following day's

activities. It was a list of sights that Max barely even heard. His mind was too occupied by the prospect of the work they had to do that night. Tomorrow seemed an impossibly long time in the future. He couldn't even imagine what it might bring.

The others finished their meals. The cadets and their guides scraped their chairs back and arranged to meet at 8 o'clock the following morning. Then they all headed off to their rooms.

The cadets' corridor was quiet. Max's heart was thumping hard as he approached his room. The cadets watched him bend down to examine the superglued hair at the bottom of the doorframe. It was still stuck at either end, but had broken in the middle. 'Somebody's been in here,' he said.

Nobody said anything. Max's palms were clammy with fear. He listened at the door. There was no sound. He inserted his key and unlocked it. Then he stepped inside.

The room was empty. Max headed straight for the bed and stood on it. He examined the second hair. Each end was firmly stuck to the ceiling panels. Whoever had been in his room, they hadn't thought to search up there.

The other cadets were waiting. He gave them a nervous thumbs-up then followed them back out into the corridor. They each examined their doors. 'Someone's been in my room too,' Lukas whispered.

'And mine,' said Lili.

And Abby's. And Sami's.

But the ceiling panels were untouched. The cadets were under surveillance, but their gear had remained hidden.

So far so good.

Kind of.

'Ten o'clock,' Max whispered to the others as they congregated in the corridor. 'That's when we'll head to the fifth floor. Until then, stay in your rooms.'

The cadets nodded solemnly. Max returned to his room and locked it from the inside. Then he checked his watch.

Ten past eight. Less than two hours to go.

8

The Fifth Floor

Time check: 21:45 hours.

The hotel was silent. Suspiciously silent. The only sound, as Max sat on the edge of his bed, was the occasional creak from the building. And then a soft knock.

It was Lukas. His face was serious. He had his black dive bag slung over his shoulders. 'It's nearly time,' he whispered.

Max felt his stomach lurch. He immediately noticed that Lukas was wearing black neoprene dive shoes instead of ordinary footwear.

'I couldn't get my shoes on over them,' he said, as if challenging Max to criticise him. Max knew better than to do that.

'Is Lili ready?' he said.

'Are any of us?' Lukas said. 'You and me first. Sami and Abby will follow in ten minutes. Lili has the optics. She'll be watching from her hotel window. But she'll scout the way to the fifth floor for us first.'

'Give me a minute,' Max said, and closed the door. He stood on his bed, removed the panel in the ceiling and hauled down his own dive bag, the handgun, chain cutters and his welding kit. He opened the bag and removed the wetsuit and neoprene dive shoes, which were rolled and stowed in an outer pocket. He took off his clothes, pulled on the tight wetsuit then replaced his clothes over the top. He put on the dive shoes and just managed to cram his feet back into his ordinary shoes. It was uncomfortable, but he wouldn't have to put up with it for long. He stowed the gun into the empty pocket of the dive bag and slung it over his shoulder. He picked up the bag containing the welding unit and chain cutters and opened the door again.

Lukas was nowhere to be seen. Max locked his room and moved along the corridor to Lili's room. He knocked and said quietly, 'It's me. Max.' There was the sound of the door being unlocked then opened. Lili let him in. She was chewing her lower lip nervously. At the window, there was a tripod with a high-powered spotting-scope with night-vision capability. It was pointing at the barge on the river. Max glanced at Pyongyang. The same patches of the city were illuminated while others weren't. It was clear that electricity was scarce.

'Are you ready?' he asked Lili.

'I feel bad,' she said. 'I should be entering the river with the rest of you.'

'Your job is at least as dangerous,' said Max. 'If not more. Don't let them catch you with this.' He indicated the spotting-scope then turned to Lukas. 'You have the GPS equipment?'

Lukas nodded.

'Then we'd better go.'

Before Lili left the room, she removed a small make-up mirror from her wash bag. Holding it, she walked to both ends of the corridor and used the mirror to check there was nobody round either corner. She gestured at Max and Lukas to follow her. Lukas used her key to lock her bedroom. They jogged towards her. Lukas handed over her key. Lili turned the corner and headed to a door further along on the right. She opened it, looked through and nodded at Max and Lukas. They followed.

They were in a concrete stairwell. They headed down, Lili scouting each floor in advance and rapping three times on the wall to indicate it was safe for them to descend with their gear. Between each floor, there was a half landing where the stairs turned back on themselves. On each of these half landings was a cupboard. Max checked the first one, to see nothing but mops and cleaning equipment. Good places to hide, he thought, if they needed to. But they met nobody on the eighth floor, nor on the seventh. When Lili reached the sixth floor, she signalled up at them to follow. But they had just reached the half landing when she let out a gasp. 'Hwan!' they heard her say.

'Lili?' Hwan said. Even though Max couldn't see the young Korean man, he could tell he was out of breath. 'Who else is there?'

Max moved as slowly and silently as possible. He unslung his dive bag from his shoulder, put the welding kit bag on the floor, then indicated to Lukas that he should hide all three bags in the cleaning cupboard. Then he continued down the stairs. Hwan and Lili were standing opposite each other, just next to the door that led on to the fifth floor There was an uncomfortable silence. Max endeavoured to give Hwan an easy smile. 'We thought you'd be in bed,' he said as he approached them.

'I . . . I was,' Hwan stammered. 'But then I got called down to reception. Somebody saw you give me your food. You must not do that again. I am in trouble for accepting it.'

'Right,' Max said carefully. 'I'll remember that. I'm sorry, I just thought –'

'I know,' Hwan said.

'Look, mate,' Max told him, 'we just wanted to have a peek around. You won't tell anybody, will you? We're just being nosy.'

Hwan frowned. 'You should not be like that,' he said quietly. 'Not here.' He glanced sidelong at the door to the fifth floor. 'This is out of bounds,' he said. 'You understand?'

Lili put her hand on the handle and rattled it. 'Locked,' she said.

'Yes,' Hwan agreed. He pointed up the stairwell. 'I must go,' he said. He frowned again. 'If anybody asks, I have not seen you. But you should return to your rooms.'

'We will,' Max said. 'I promise.'

Hwan continued up the stairwell. Lukas was standing there silently. Hwan looked him up and down, but said nothing as he passed and continued up the stairwell and out of sight.

Max was sweating badly as Hwan's footsteps faded away.

'Can we trust him?' Lili said.

'I think so. We don't have much choice. It's that or abort the mission. Can you get that door open?'

Lili didn't answer but removed a set of tension wrenches from her pocket while Max moved up the stairs again. Lukas had retrieved their gear from the cleaning cupboard. By the time they'd carried the bags downstairs, Lili had opened the door to the fifth floor. 'Good luck,' she whispered.

'Get the others down here as quickly as possible,' Max said as they slipped through the door. They heard her locking it behind them.

It was pitch dark, with the stale smell of disuse. Max and Lukas stayed still for a moment, listening hard for any sound of movement. There was none.

'They packed me a torch,' Lukas whispered. He switched it on, keeping his hand over the bulb to restrict the light, and played the narrow beam around the space.

A face seemed to jump out at Max from the darkness. He started, but calmed himself as he realised it was a propaganda poster on the far wall of this large room. It was the same poster of the Supreme Leader he'd seen all around the city. The whole room was plastered with these propaganda pictures, like some spooky old museum.

'Weird,' Lukas muttered.

'Right,' Max said. He pointed towards a corridor in the far corner. 'That way,' he said, remembering the layout of the plans Hector had shown them. They crossed the room and moved along the corridor. It was plastered with more propaganda pictures. On the left there was an opening leading into another room. Curious, they looked inside. It was empty, but one wall was covered with TV monitors, and another with desks of listening equipment. It seemed rather old-fashioned. 'I bet they used to use the fifth floor for surveillance,' Max whispered. 'They probably have more sophisticated ways now, but I guess that explains why they don't want anybody poking around here.'

Lukas grunted his agreement and led them away from the surveillance room. They came to a second door on the right. It creaked as they opened it. They found themselves in what might have once been a store room. There were empty shelves on two walls, and a number of wicker baskets dotted around. On the far wall was a square opening: the laundry chute. They approached it. Lukas shone his torch down the hole. It was a sheer drop, with no sign of the bottom.

'Kill the light while we wait for the others,' Max said.

Lukas switched off his torch. The two cadets crouched beneath the opening to the laundry chute and waited silently.

Five minutes passed.

Ten.

Then they heard a noise. Saw the flash of a torch beam. Max felt himself tensing up as figures appeared. He squinted. Could he recognise the outlines of Sami and Abby? They were behind the torchlight so it was impossible to tell. But as the torch illuminated the two crouching cadets, he heard Abby's voice.

'Sheesh, did you see that room with all the surveillance equipment?' she whispered. 'What kind of place is this?'

The kind of place, Max thought, where the punishment if they were caught would be severe.

'Did anyone see you?'

'No,' Sami replied. 'But Lili said you met Hwan.'

'I think it'll be okay,' Max said.

'Are you sure? If he tells someone . . .'

'He's got nothing to tell. Only that he found us wandering round the hotel. Come on, let's get to work.'

Abby and Sami had more gear than Max and Lukas. In addition to their dive bags, they each had a holdall. Sami's contained the abseiling gear, Abby's the second underwater welding kit. The abseiling gear comprised a long coil of rope, a harness and a steel bar, somewhat wider than the laundry chute opening. Max had more experience of abseiling than the others. It had been his skill in this discipline that had brought him to the attention of the Special Forces Cadets in the first place. Leaving his welding unit on the ground, he donned the harness and clipped himself to the rope. He positioned the metal bar so it lay across the opening, then climbed into the chute. He nodded at the others, who were still lit up by torchlight, then started to lower himself down the chute.

The first few metres, while there was still a little light from above, were the easiest. After that, it became dark and horribly cramped. The dive bag on his back pressed against the back of the laundry chute. It stopped Max from falling too fast, but it made him claustrophobic. It felt as though the walls were pressing in on him in the darkness. He had to breathe deeply to keep himself from panicking.

He continued to descend in the blackness, unsure how far he'd come or how long he had taken. Now and then he heard voices as the laundry chute passed behind the walls of occupied rooms. Here he moved with the utmost care, reducing his speed by half and keeping as silent as possible. And though it grew colder the further he descended, he was drenched in sweat. Part of that was because he wore a wetsuit under his clothes. Part of it was raw fear.

The bottom of the chute arrived suddenly. There was no light to announce it. He simply fell backwards where there was no back wall to support his dive bag. He tumbled painfully on to a cold concrete floor. There was a smell of damp and something else – something foetid. A rustling noise surrounded him. He didn't want to think what was making that sound. In the darkness, he unclipped himself from the rope, then tugged on it three times. Almost immediately he felt it sliding out of his grasp as one of the other cadets pulled it back up the chute.

Max stood in the complete darkness, listening to the scurrying sounds. His skin prickled. The damp air caught in his lungs. He waited. Ten minutes later he heard something moving down the laundry chute. He switched on his torch to see the two bags containing the underwater welding units land on the floor. He untied them, then allowed the rope to be pulled back up.

The next delivery was a cadet: Abby. She was pale-faced and sweating. For once, she had no wisecracks. Her attention, like Max's, was grabbed by the sudden blurred movement of rodents, scared by the light, into the corners of the dank basement.

The rope disappeared again. They waited in tense silence for the next cadet. Max looked around the basement. There was a door against one wall, but he didn't think anyone had been in here for years. It was crumbling with neglect, the floor thick with rat droppings. He felt like he was inhaling poison.

Sami arrived next. Max recognised his friend's trainers as they appeared at the bottom of the laundry chute. Sami had managed to descend with his dive bag and his holdall, and he was sweating furiously as a result. He took in the basement with a glance and did not seem as concerned by the environment as the others. Max reminded himself that, in another life, Sami had spent a long time living in poor conditions.

The rope disappeared again. It seemed to take an age for Lukas to descend. In reality? Five minutes. His neoprene shoes announced his arrival. Max blinked at them as a worrying though hit him. When Lukas emerged from the laundry chute, he said, 'Did Hwan see your shoes?'

Lukas, sweating, looked down at his feet. 'What?'

'You're the only one of us who didn't manage to get their regular shoes over their dive shoes. Did Hwan see?'

'I don't think so.'

'You don't *think* so?' Max's voice had an edge. He couldn't help it.

'Back off, Max.'

Sami stepped in. There was something about the disappointed expression on his honest, open face that made Max and Lukas fall silent. He took hold of the rope. 'This had better still be here when we get back.' He gave it a tug to check it was still firmly anchored at the top of the laundry chute. His eyes widened as he pulled away more slack than he expected. 'Oh no,' he whispered. 'No, no, no . . .'

There was a clattering, echoing sound from the top of the chute. The cadets winced as the ring of the iron bar bashing against the sides of the chute grew louder and louder. It sounded to Max as if it must surely be audible to everyone in the hotel. After a few seconds it crashed to the ground. The rodents squeaked in fright as they scattered into the dark corners of the basement.

Then silence.

The cadets stared at each other.

'Well,' Abby said, giving the boys a steady look, 'I'd say this is all going swimmingly, wouldn't you?'

9

The Sewer

Time check: 23:05 hours.

The cadets moved quickly, stripping off their outer clothes to reveal their wetsuits. The metal bar falling had made everything more urgent.

'I think the chute might be narrow enough for us to use an old mountaineering trick called chimneying when we want to get back up,' Max said as they changed. 'What you do is, you put your back against one wall, your feet against the opposite –'

'Tell you what, Max,' Abby said. 'Why don't you explain it when there *isn't* a risk of one of those spooky hotel staff coming to find out what that noise was?'

'Roger that,' Lukas muttered.

They bundled up their clothes and placed them at the bottom of the laundry chute. Then they shouldered their dive bags and moved across the basement. According to the plans of the hotel, there was a panel in the floor against the wall opposite the chute. It meant swiping away a thick layer of rodent droppings with their feet. Abby was the one to find it. She knelt down and dug her fingernails under the edge of the panel. She managed to raise it a tiny bit, but it was heavy and it took the strength all four of the cadets to shift it.

The hole it revealed was just about big enough for a person to squeeze through. They could hear liquid trickling below, and there was an overpowering stench that made Max retch. Lukas shone his torch into the hole. It wasn't a big drop – a couple of metres at the most – but it was a distinctly unappealing one. A stream of human waste ran below them, glistening and foetid. Max caught sight of several long, slithery tails scurrying away from the torchlight. He retched again.

'You're seriously telling me we have to go down there?' Abby whispered.

The cadets peered into the hole again. 'It is the most disgusting thing I have ever seen,' Sami said earnestly. He looked at Max, wide-eyed. 'You go first.'

'What? Why me?'

'Because you are definitely the bravest,' Sami said. His expression was serious, but Max had the feeling his friend was just trying to flatter him.

'I'll do it,' Lukas said. Without waiting for a reply, he lowered himself into the hole, gripping his torch between his teeth. 'Oh, man,' he said. His voice echoed against the stone walls of the sewer. 'This Prospero dude better be grateful.'

Lukas moved along the sewer to give the others room. Max went next. As he lowered himself, he felt his neoprene-clad foot press down on something soft and squishy. He winced again, unwilling to look down. Then he made the mistake of breathing in through his nose. The smell was fouler than anything he'd ever experienced. He clamped one hand over his face, but had to release it again as Sami passed him one of the underwater welding kit bags. Sensing Abby and Sami behind him, he tapped Lukas on the back and pointed along the sewer to get him moving.

It was slippery underfoot. Max trod carefully. The last thing he wanted to do was trip. Nor did he want to come into contact with the walls or ceiling. They were close to his skin – there was very little room down here – and covered in a damp, sticky substance Max didn't want to investigate further, and certainly didn't want to touch.

Something dripped on to his face. He wiped it off quickly, but didn't dare check the back of his hand to see what it was.

There was a constant, high-pitched squeak of rodents. Max was aware of them scurrying in the tunnel, their shadows changing shape in the moving torchlight. Now and then he felt something brush against his feet. He didn't want to know what it was.

Max knew from the plans Hector had shown them that the sewer tunnel was about fifty metres long. It felt like twice that. He kept expecting to get used to the stench, but he didn't. If anything, it grew worse, and with it grew his claustrophobia. He wanted to shout out, or run, but he couldn't do either. All he could do was press on, weighed down by his dive bag, oppressed by his squalid surroundings . . .

Time dragged. Max felt as if he'd been in the sewer for an hour, but a glance at his watch told him it was only 23:20 hours. They'd barely been down here for ten minutes.

He nearly slipped on something soft, and cursed under his breath. Then he gritted his teeth and continued walking along the stinking, revolting tunnel. The next time he checked his watch, it was 23:35 hours.

'Jeez . . .' Abby gasped from behind him. 'How much further?'

'I dunno,' Max said, his teeth gritted. Even as he said it, he caught a whiff of something. It wasn't fresh air, exactly, but it was a little less foul. 'Not far, I don't think.'

He was right. With each step they took, the air cleared a little. The sewer grew wider. Max felt a breeze.

'I can see something,' Lukas announced. Max peered past him, squinting in the semi-darkness. Sure enough, up ahead, there was a wall with a grille set in it. Moonlight streamed in through the holes in the grille. The stream of effluent was channelled into a hole at the end of the tunnel. They were able to step out of the stream and walk alongside it.

'I don't ever want to do that again,' Sami said.

'We've got to get back yet,' Max told him. He approached the grille – it was rusty and grimy – and looked through it. They were just above the river. Immediately below them was a pipe discharging the sewage into the water. It extended for about a metre. From this height they would be able to jump past it. But first they had to remove the grille.

Sami, who was in charge of one of the welding kits, started to unpack it. Their plan was to burn a hole in the grille, then push themselves through. But Max told Sami to wait. He could see that the mortar around the grille was old and crumbling. He put his fingers through the holes in the grille and pulled. It immediately came loose. Lukas did the same on the other side of the grille and, in a matter of seconds, they managed to pull it away from the wall. The cadets crowded round the open cavity, breathing in lungfuls of fresh air.

Max could just make out the lights of the prison barge along the river. Weirdly, it seemed closer than it had done from the ninth floor. Max knew that was just a trick of perspective. It was going to be a long, difficult swim. 'We can't hang around,' he said.

The cadets got to work. Lukas prepared the GPS equipment. On the flight to Beijing, Woody had given him detailed instructions about how to do this. Regular GPS signals did not work underwater, but they had an alternative.

'You'll have a GPS gateway unit,' Woody had said. 'You attach it to a fixed point and let it float in the river. It communicates with GPS satellites. Then you each have a wrist unit. The wrist units communicate with the gateway unit using acoustic signals that can propagate underwater. They'll tell you your exact position as well as your depth and each other's positions, which will appear as blue dots. This wrist units will have the location of the prison barge pre-loaded. It'll appear as a red dot. You just have to follow that – the display will tell you how many metres you are from the target.'

'And we couldn't have had one of those in the lake?' Lukas had said.

'What would be the fun in that, big fella?' Woody had winked at him.

Now, Lukas was unpacking the gateway unit. It had a waterproof case, three thick black antennae, and was attached to a lanyard several metres long. Lukas tied one end of the lanyard to the metal grille, which they had propped up against the wall, then powered up the unit. Its face glowed. Lukas lowered it by the lanyard into the river. When it hit the water, the current pulled it downstream. The lanyard became taut. Lukas gave each cadet a wrist unit. Max clipped his to his left wrist. The face was much larger than a regular watch and it had two buttons. One was a panic button: if activated, it would alert the others that the wearer was in distress. The other was a power button. Max pressed it and the face of his unit lit up. It displayed a great deal of information: time, depth, temperature, position. It took a few seconds to connect to the gateway unit. When it did, a red dot appeared. That was the barge. That was their objective.

The cadets donned their rebreathing gear. Max and Abby strapped their welding units to a chest harness. Sami secreted his sat phone in a waterproof pouch and inserted this into a tight wetsuit pocket. Max checked that the handgun was safe and did the same, then clipped the chain cutters to the chest harness. They stashed their empty dive bags by the sewage stream. Then they turned to each other.

'Okay,' Max said. 'Let's recap on the plan. We swim in pairs. Lukas and I will go first. Abby and Sami, follow after about a minute.'

'Don't you love it when he takes charge?' Abby said. But her wisecrack fell flat. Maybe it was something to do with the tremor in her voice.

'We head for the barge in as straight a line as possible,' Max continued. 'If we meet another boat, we avoid it by diving deeper. We only break the surface in an absolute emergency. Once Lukas and I are at the prison barge, I'll use the welding kit to burn a hole in the hull and scuttle it. Hopefully, that will give Prospero the opportunity to escape. I'll hand over the weapon, and our job is done. Any problems, Lukas and I will swim to Sami and Abby's position. Sami has the second welding kit, so he can have another go at breaching the hull if I don't manage it for any reason. Once that's done, we return to the hotel. We get out of our dirty wetsuits, into our clean clothes, chimney up the laundry chute . . .'

'. . . looking forward to that,' Abby said.

'. . . and we're in bed by dawn.' He looked out towards the river again. 'I'm making it sound simple, right?'

Nobody spoke.

'Any major problems – and I mean problems that threaten to compromise the mission – we activate the panic buttons on our wrist units. If that happens, we all return immediately to this location.'

'If we can,' Lukas said.

'Yeah,' Max agreed. 'If we can.'

'I am very scared,' Sami said.

'Me too,' said Abby.

'Same,' said Lukas.

'We'd be crazy if we weren't,' Max said. His stomach was turning over and his limbs were cold. 'Remember,' he said, 'nobody knows we're coming or what we're doing. We have the element of surprise.' He checked his wrist unit. 'It's one minute to midnight,' he said. 'Let's make a start.'

He clambered over the ledge and prepared to jump.

10

Panic

The water was colder than Max expected. There was a warm stream where the effluent from the sewage pipe merged with the river water, but Max avoided that with a shudder. He swam away from the island with three powerful strokes, then concentrated on depth. Four metres down would be enough, he decided.

It was entirely dark. The moonlight didn't penetrate the water, and blackness seemed to press in on him. Max could barely see his hand when he held it just in front of his mask. His wrist unit glowed faintly. It was the only way he could navigate, or even orientate himself. The red dot that indicated the prison barge was on the top edge of the display. The blue dots that showed the other cadets were clustered on the bottom edge.

He heard a muffled, bubbly splash. A few seconds later, there was a tap on his shoulder. He twisted round to see an indistinct shadow he assumed was Lukas. He tapped his mate on the arm in return, then twisted again in what he thought was the direction of the barge, and swam.

Lukas stuck close. Even with the wrist units, it would be hard to locate each other underwater if they became separated. Max really didn't want that to happen. This was nothing like the lake swim they'd undertaken in training. The current was strong. It seemed to pull the energy out of Max's muscles. The welding unit was heavy and made movement more difficult. He was strong and fit, but this was going to be a true challenge.

After thirty seconds it was clear they had the direction wrong. The current was knocking them off-track and the red dot was gradually circling the face of the wrist unit. As one, Max and Lukas readjusted their trajectory. It meant swimming into the current at a steeper angle, which in turn made the dive a tougher prospect. Max steeled himself for a long, gruelling swim.

It almost felt like they weren't moving. As they were practically blind, they had nothing to measure their progress against. All they could do was rely on their wrist units, which showed them approaching the barge at a painfully slow rate. After fifteen minutes, they'd barely covered half the distance. After thirty, their rate seemed to have slowed even further. Max's muscles burned and he realised he was panting through the rebreather as his tiring body called for more oxygen.

He had just checked the time again – 00:44 hours – when the hull of a boat appeared right in front of them, moving fast. Max and Lukas pulled back in panic as the hull slid past them in a cloud of bubbles and murky river water. The cadets peered at each other through the gloom. Lukas would surely be thinking the same as him. Any closer and they'd have been hit by the hull. Chance of survival? Practically zero. He checked his wrist unit. He'd been so focused on the red dot, he'd stopped paying attention to the depth gauge. They were only two metres from the surface. They needed to get lower.

Max's heart was thumping as he and Lukas moved to a depth of five metres. He felt the pressure build up in his ears. A glance at his wrist gauge told him that Sami and Abby were still together, but well behind them. He hoped they were staying deep too. It was the only way they could be sure of avoiding a collision.

Distance to the target: thirty metres. They powered forward. Max was beginning to wish he'd eaten more at dinner. Energy was leaching from his body. He was finding it difficult to keep up with Lukas. But he kept going. There was no turning back now.

Distance: twenty metres. Max sensed a vessel passing overhead and felt the disturbance of the current. It occurred to him that, whatever the vessel was, it was close to the barge. Too close? Had the authorities felt the need to increase the security around the boat? Did they know someone was coming to make a rescue attempt?

Fifteen metres. Lukas was right by him. He still couldn't see the barge in the dark water. Instinctively, he touched the underwater welding kit clipped to his chest, preparing himself to make use of it.

Ten metres.

That was when it happened.

Was it the noise he heard first? A piercing, wailing siren, muffled under the water but still loud. Or did he see the lights, so bright above the river that they illuminated the almost impenetrable gloom? He knew, instantly, that they were spotlights, several of them, directed towards the water surrounding the barge and moving in a criss-cross pattern. He twisted round to look at Lukas, whose response was identical to Max's. They each slammed the panic button on their wrist units. The units vibrated. The screens turned red for a second. Then they shut down. In a rush of panic, Max unclipped the welding unit from his chest. He needed to move fast, and it was a hindrance. As soon as he let go of it, it sank to the bottom of the river. Max realised suddenly that he'd made a terrible error. The welding unit wasn't just a cutting tool. It could have been a weapon, and now it was lost.

Big, big mistake. Because just then then the divers arrived.

Max felt like he was back at the lake near Valley House, surrounded by the Watchers. But he soon realised that Hector, Woody and Angel had gone easy on them. It was impossible to tell how many frogmen there were. All Max knew was that they were numerous – and aggressive. He felt an iron fist in his stomach, and an elbow cracked against his right cheek. The rebreather mask was ripped from his face, surrounding him in a fierce underwater cloud of bubbles. An arm grabbed him from behind, clutching his throat. And the pressure in his ears decreased as his attackers forced him to the surface.

Max broke through into the open air with a noisy gasp. A searchlight shone from the boat directly into his face, blinding him. All he could hear was shouting: angry, aggressive Korean voices, some of them screaming at him from very close, others from further away, perhaps on the barge. He heard Lukas yelling his name, but his mate's voice was becoming more distant. They were plainly being separated.

The immediate shock of the attack wore off. Max started to struggle, to flail about with his arms. Bad move. He took another blow in the face. And another. He started to feel woozy. The burst of energy from the adrenaline rush was ebbing away. He swallowed a mouthful of river water and coughed violently, his head still spinning.

He tried to call out Lukas's name, but his voice wasn't working. He felt like he was drowning. He felt another blow to the stomach. Another to the head.

He passed out.

When he woke – seconds, minutes or hours later – he was no longer in the water. He was lying on something hard. His head throbbed. Somebody had their hand around his throat. They were screaming into his face, but his vision was blurred and he couldn't see them.

There was nothing on his back. His rebreathing apparatus must have been removed. But he was still wet, so he couldn't be long out of the water. He tried to inhale. It was difficult because of the hand round his throat, but he managed half a noisy lungful. His vision cleared a little. An angry uniformed North Korean official was right in front of him, shouting incomprehensibly. Max tried to work out where he was. He appeared to be on the deck of a boat. The prison barge? He assumed so. The official swiped him round the face, which seemed to make him even angrier. He held up the back of his hand to show that it was covered in blood. His own blood. Max could feel it flooding from his nose.

He was pulled up to his knees. His eyes rolled and he almost collapsed again. But he managed to stay upright. There were five or six officials. Maybe more. Some of them were speaking on mobile phones. All of them were looking in Max's direction. He was aware of searchlights on the deck. They were pointing at the river, zigzagging in a random search pattern.

Searching for others.

Lukas had been captured. He had to be – he had been right by Max. His thoughts turned to Abby and Sami. What was their location? Were they safe? Did they know what was happening? Max and Lukas had hit their panic buttons, and they had agreed that this was a sign they should return to the island. But would they act on that? *Could* they act on it?

More thoughts crowded into his head. How had their attackers known they were coming? Had he and Lukas tripped some sort of intruder alert? It didn't seem likely. He hadn't noticed any cables in the water – and anyway, such alerts would be activated by river fish. But there was only one other option: the Korean authorities were expecting them. How? Had somebody tipped them off?

Who?

Max was in no position to worry about it any longer.

Yet another blow to the head knocked him back down to the deck.

He was out cold.

Abby and Sami's wrist units had vibrated simultaneously. They immediately stopped swimming and instinctively locked arms so they didn't become separated by the current. Their faces almost touching, they stared at each other through the dark water in alarm. It was a look that said: what's happening? What do we do?

The faces of their wrist units had turned red. They stared at them. The blue dots that indicated Max and Lukas were almost exactly on top of the red dot of the barge. Then, as if somebody had switched off a light, they disappeared. Either their units were broken, or someone had switched them off.

Their instructions were clear: in the event of anyone activating the panic alarm, they were to return to the hotel immediately. They nodded at each other, twisted around in the water and powered back the way they came.

But it was apparent within seconds that their way was blocked. Searchlights pierced the water above them. The hulls of three boats passed above them. Sami even thought he caught a glimpse of other divers up ahead. Abby must have seen them too, because she grabbed his arm and pointed in a different direction. She was obviously thinking the same as Sami. They were compromised. Somebody knew about them. And it seemed that the way back to the hotel was likely to be under heavy surveillance.

They needed to see what was happening. They couldn't

do that underwater, but breaking the surface here would be madness. They had to head for the river's edge, where they could surface in the shadow and camouflage of the high bank. And they had to do it now.

Side by side, they cut through the water, away from the searchlights and the shadowy figures of the other divers. When they reached the river wall – algae-covered and slimy – they hesitated. Even here, breaking the surface was a risk. But it was one they had to take. They nodded at each other and slowly raised their heads above water.

The sight made them sick. Five or six boats surrounded the prison barge, each with a couple of high-powered searchlights beaming down into the water. More boats had established a cordon around the hotel island, making access impossible for Abby and Sami. Worst of all, the prison barge was moving. It had unmoored from the pier and was slowly sliding downstream.

They removed their rebreathing masks. 'You think Max and Lukas are on the barge?' Abby said breathlessly.

Sami gave a solemn nod. 'I am absolutely certain they are,' he said. 'The boat is moving already. There wouldn't have been time to get them off.'

'Then what do we do?'

'I don't know.' He turned his head and stared back at the hotel. 'Lili,' he said.

Abby swore under her breath. 'Somebody knew about us. It means they'll be coming for her too, but maybe they're not there yet. We have to warn her.' She fumbled in her wetsuit pocket for the sat phone. Lili had the other one. 'I'm going to call her,' Abby said. 'Tell her to get out of the hotel.' She swore again. 'I can't get a signal,' she said. 'What are we going to do?'

There was panic in her voice, and for good reason. Two of them had been captured, and if Lili didn't move fast, the North Koreans could make that three.

11

1313

Time check: 00:45 hours.

Lili watched with sick horror as events unfolded on the river.

At first, everything had seemed okay. By which Lili meant, nothing had changed. There was no sign of her fellow cadets. No sign of increased activity on the prison barge. Through her high-powered night-vision scope, she could clearly see a guard on the deck of the boat, but he had his back to her and was looking in the opposite direction.

It had all changed at five minutes past eleven. The river, dark and sluggish, had suddenly lit up. Several high-powered boats appeared from the direction of the hotel island, speeding urgently towards the prison barge, bright searchlights pointing down into the water. Two searchlights blazed on the prison barge itself, and suddenly there were more guards on deck – too many for Lili to count as they were all running around. She could hear them shouting at each other.

Then she saw something that made her blood freeze. Two people were being fished out of the river and hauled onto the barge. She couldn't make out their faces at this distance, but it didn't take a genius to work out who they were. Max and Lukas. Captured.

She scanned the river, searching for Sami and Abby. There was no sign of them. What did that mean? Were they safe? Where were they?

Lili was not a panicky kind of person. When something went wrong, she was more likely to keep calm and think her way through the problem than to overreact and lose her head. She was a good fighter, she was strong. But she was also smart, and she knew that when it was a choice between brains or brawn, brains normally won.

But it was hard not to panic. She drew away from the scope, aware that her pulse had risen and her breath was coming in short gasps. She had an overwhelming urge to run and hide. But where? She was alone, in a strange and hostile country. She didn't know what to do.

Think, Lili, she told herself. She put her hands to her head and forced herself to breathe. *Think . . . What is your next move?*

Her room was locked from the inside, but she suddenly felt like she was in a prison of her own making. If the authorities knew about Max and Lukas, she was, of course, under suspicion herself. It meant they were coming for her. Right now. She had to get out of there. Quickly.

There was no time to dismantle the scope. She left it on its tripod pointing out over the river. It was incriminating, but she had no time and no choice. Her satellite phone lay on the bed next to a pair of binoculars that had been supplied as an additional surveillance tool and the make-up mirror she had used to check round corners on the way to the fifth floor. She stuffed the sat phone into a pocket, grabbed the binoculars and the make-up mirror and unlocked the door. She took a deep breath, opened up and peered outside.

The corridor was empty. She turned right and ran along it until it turned right. She held out the mirror to check round the corner.

Her heart nearly stopped.

Four men in military uniform were marching along the corridor towards her. They were armed with pistols, holstered on the outside of their jackets. Their faces were severe. They weren't far off, and they were moving briskly.

Lili ran like lightning. Her feet made almost no noise as she sprinted back past her room to the other end of the corridor. Here there was another corner. She glanced over her shoulder before she took it, just in time to see the boots of one of the military men appear round the opposite corner. Once she'd turned right, she pressed her back up against the wall and used her mirror to watch the four guards. They marched up to her door. One of them thumped on it three times with his fist. She didn't need to see any more. She wasn't out of danger yet. She sprinted down the empty corridor, turned right again at the end and found herself by the stairwell. Her instinct was to go down, into the reception area and out of the hotel, where she could lose herself in the streets of Pyongyang. She even started following the staircase down.

But then she stopped.

Think.

How had her friends been captured? The river was wide and deep. Max and Lukas were small in comparison. The chances of them being located by chance were tiny. Which meant the Korean authorities knew they were coming. They *knew* Max and Lukas would be in the water, in the vicinity of the prison barge. How? Had somebody tipped them off? Who could that be? Jerry and Elsa? That would make no sense. They would be in as much trouble with the authorities as the cadets themselves, if they were accused of smuggling agents across the border. Maybe somebody had seen them switch suitcases at the airport. But that wouldn't explain how Max and Lukas had been located in the river.

She realised she instinctively knew what the answer was, even before logic led her there. The only other possibility was Hwan. He had seen Lili leading Max and Lukas to the fifth floor. He hadn't seen their diving gear, but . . . She sighed. Lukas's neoprene dive shoes had been visible. If Hwan had told the authorities about those, they'd have worked it out immediately.

Her eyes narrowed. The safety of her fellow cadets was down to her. If Hwan had betrayed them, she had to find out what he had told the authorities before she decided on her next move. She was already heading upstairs before the thought was fully formed in her mind: she had to find Hwan, and ask him.

Lili's memory was unusually good. 'Photographic', some people called it, but that wasn't quite accurate. She just had excellent recall. So she remembered quite clearly that as Jerry had handed out keys in reception, he had told Hwan his room number was 1313. It was late, so he'd most likely be there.

She took the steps two at a time, constantly scanning the stairwell above for any sign of threatening personnel. But the corridors were deserted at this hour and she was soon on the thirteenth floor. Sweat prickled on her forehead as she moved from the stairwell to the corridor. She could hear people arguing in a nearby bedroom, but her route to room 1313 took her in the opposite direction, and the voices faded. When she reached Hwan's room, she stood by the door, listening carefully. She couldn't hear any voices but she could, perhaps, hear somebody moving around inside.

She raised her fist to knock. As she did so, she remembered Jerry's comment as he'd handed Hwan his key. *1313, unlucky for some . . .*

Unlucky for her? She was about to find out.

Gently, she knocked three times.

The sound of movement inside the room stopped. There was silence, then the sound of footsteps. Lili realised she was holding her breath. She forced herself to breathe.

The door opened a crack. Hwan's thin, anxious face appeared. He blinked, obviously surprised to see Lili. 'What do you want?' he said. He sounded unusually aggressive.

'We need to talk,' Lili replied.

Hwan tried to shut the door, but he couldn't: Lili's right foot was over the threshold, and it wasn't going anywhere.

'Please,' Hwan mouthed silently. 'Go!'

Lili shook her head. Hwan bowed his, as if in defeat. He opened up and she stepped inside.

And she realised, as Hwan closed the door behind her, that she had made a terrible mistake. Hwan was not alone. There was another Korean man in here. He wore black trousers and a black T-shirt. He wore a shoulder holster. It was empty. The pistol it normally carried was in his hand, and it was aimed at Lili.

Nobody moved. Then the gunman said, 'Sit down.' With his handgun he indicated the bed. Lili reluctantly moved to the edge of the bed and sat down. The gunman stood directly in front of her, while Hwan retreated to one corner of the room. He looked wretched, helpless and scared. The gunman stared down at Lili with a dismissive expression. He clearly didn't see Lili as a threat, because he re-holstered his handgun before cracking his knuckles.

'I work for the Ministry of State Security,' he said in excellent English. 'Do you know what that is?'

Lili wordlessly shook her head.

'It is the secret police. We report directly to the Supreme Leader. We have a special place close by where we take enemies of the state. Would you like to know what happens there?'

Lili didn't reply.

He carried on regardless. 'All prisoners are . . .' – he hesitated, before putting an unpleasant emphasis on his next word – '*questioned*. Sometimes they even survive the questioning. But whether they survive or not, they always – *always* – tell us what we want to know. Would you like to pay it a visit?'

Lili shook her head again.

'I thought not. In that case, I suggest you tell me everything

I want to know right now. Let us start with a simple question. What is your name?'

'Annabel,' she said.

The man bent down so his face was close to hers. 'You are a nasty, lying little girl,' he said.

Lili fixed him with a calm stare. When she spoke, it was in little more than a whisper. 'I might be a nasty, lying little girl,' she said. 'But I am a nasty, lying little girl with a black belt in four martial arts.'

And before the man had the opportunity to speak again, Lili hooked her left foot around his ankle. She yanked his leg from underneath him while striking him hard in the breastbone with the heel of her hand. He collapsed with a heavy thump, by which time Lili was already sitting on his legs. She clenched her right fist, allowing the knuckle of her middle finger to protrude. She briefly sized the man up, then delivered a sharp, shocking blow to his kidneys. The man's eyes bulged with the sudden pain of being winded. He coughed, then struggled to catch his breath. Lili grabbed his handgun from his holster. With practised ease, she cocked the weapon and held it steadily, aiming it at the man's face. 'Speak another word,' she said, 'and you know what will happen.' She sounded a lot more confident than she felt.

The man nodded. Now he was unarmed and no longer in control, his sneering arrogance had left him. One-handed, Lili quickly unbuckled his belt and removed it from around his trousers.

'What are you doing?' Hwan said, his voice high-pitched and stressed.

'You, shut up,' Lili said. 'You, lie on your front.'

The secret police officer did as he was told.

'Hands behind your back,' Lili said. When he obeyed, Lili tied the belt in a figure-of-eight loop around his wrists and buckled it tightly. Then she jumped up, took a pillow from the bed and removed the pillow case. She pulled this over the police officer's head and tied a tight knot at the nape of his neck. She stood again and turned to Hwan, who was still cringing in the corner of the room. He seemed horrified at what she had done.

'Out,' she said.

Hwan swallowed hard.

'*Now!*'

He moved to the door, opened it and stepped into the corridor. Lili followed, taking the key from inside the room and locking it from the outside once she had joined Hwan. She slid the handgun behind her cardigan so it was hidden. She considered going to find Jerry and Elsa, but quickly dismissed the idea. They could be under armed guard too by now.

'This is what we're going to do,' she said. 'You and me, we're heading to reception. Once we're there, we're going to walk straight out of the hotel. I'll be behind you every step of the way, and you know what I'm carrying. Don't make the mistake of thinking I won't use it if you raise the alarm.'

She thought Hwan might cry. 'You don't understand . . .'

'I understand that my friends are in trouble. Trust me, I'll do anything to help them. *Anything*. Do you understand?'

Hwan nodded. Lili glanced back towards room 1313. Unlucky for some, she thought. But the belt and pillowcase wouldn't hold the secret police guy for long. And if he raised the alarm, her chance of getting out of here was zero. She checked the time. 01:00 hours.

'So move,' she said. '*Now!*'

12

The Bridge

Sami and Abby could feel their temperature dropping. Their energy sapping away.

But that wasn't their biggest problem.

Their biggest problem was that the prison barge was now out of sight.

'It wasn't moving fast,' Abby said. 'It's just because we're low in the water that we can't see it.'

'It doesn't matter how slowly it's moving,' Sami said. 'If we stay still, it's getting away from us. And if Max and Lukas are on that boat . . .' His face creased up into a frown. 'Max is my best friend,'

'But we can't move,' Abby said. 'If we do . . .'

She gestured to the river. It was clear what she meant. Sami counted six boats, all of them with searchlights whose beams zigzagged across the river, searching for threats. Their wrist units no longer indicated Max and Sami's positions. If they were to follow the barge, they would have to break the surface, and they would risk being seen.

'We can't leave them,' Sami said resolutely. 'Whatever happens, we can't leave them.'

'Agreed,' Abby said. 'But what –'

'I have an idea,' Sami said.

'I'm all ears.'

Sami gave her a confused look. 'What does that mean?'

'Just tell me your idea, Sami.'

'These boats are all staying in this area. They're not following the prison barge. They don't expect anybody in the water to be able to follow it.'

'Well, they're right,' Abby said. Her voice was trembling a little with the cold.

'Yes,' Sami nodded. 'They are right. But earlier today, when we crossed the bridge on our sightseeing tour, did you notice those old wooden boats on the far side of the bridge?'

'No.'

'They are there. I think I saw Max looking at them. I think he will remember.'

'Max won't be able to get to those boats, Sami.'

'I'm not talking about Max,' Sami said. 'I'm talking about us. We can't follow the prison barge underwater – it's too cold and moving too fast. But we can follow the bank to those boats. I'm sure some of them had motors. We can steal one and follow the barge like that.'

Abby stared at him. 'You're crazy,' she said. 'They'll see us.'

'Okay, then,' Sami said. 'We'll just bob here in the water waiting for them to find us. And while we wait, we'll know that Max and Lukas –'

'All right, all right,' Abby hissed. 'I'm not saying we shouldn't do anything.'

'I'm sorry,' Sami said. 'I know you weren't.'

Abby peered across the water again. 'The boats will be locked up,' she said.

'I have the underwater welding unit.'

She nodded. 'This bank of the river is in shadow,' she said. 'I guess there's a chance that if we get to the boats, we can move without being seen. But it's a big risk, Sami. As soon as we get a connection on the sat phone, we should call the Watchers. Tell them what we're doing. Make sure they haven't made other plans.'

'Okay,' Sami said. He shivered. 'Whatever happens, we can't stay still in this water all night. It will suck the life from us.'

'Yeah,' Abby said. 'It would be a shame to let that happen and deny anyone else the pleasure.' She gave a rueful smile. 'I know it's cold, but it beats maths homework, right?' When Sami didn't smile back, she said, 'Just a joke, buddy. Come on, let's go get our friends.'

They replaced their rebreathing masks. Seconds later they were underwater and heading downstream.

Lili and Hwan's footsteps echoed as they moved down the stairwell. Lili had decided to avoid the lift again. The stairs gave them exit routes up or down. If they were caught in the lift, there was nowhere to run.

They didn't speak until they reached the ground floor. Hwan was sweating. Lili thought he might be on the verge of collapsing. She briefly considered questioning him in the concrete stairwell to find out what information he had given the authorities. But no. There would be military personnel scouring the hotel for her. They needed to get away as quickly as possible.

'Okay, Hwan,' she said. 'Remember: I'll be behind you and I'm armed.' She showed him the handgun underneath her cardigan. Hwan swallowed hard. 'We're going to walk straight across reception to the exit.'

'What if they're searching for us?' Hwan said.

'They *are* searching for us, Hwan. For you as well as me – and I've got a feeling this will end badly for both of us if we're caught. But I think they'll be concentrating on the upper levels. They won't expect us to show ourselves in public. So that's what we're going to do. And we're going to do it now. Act normal. Go.'

The way to reception was through a heavy fire door. Hwan pushed it open and looked timidly through the gap. '*Just walk!*' Lili hissed. She poked him in the back with the barrel of her gun. He twitched as if he had been electrocuted. Then he walked. Lili followed.

She knew instantly that entering the reception area had been a mistake. Like the hotel corridors, it was practically deserted. There were no guests here, just the receptionists, two men and a woman, behind the desk. Outside, Lili could see flashing neon lights.

She had a choice to make. Keep going, or turn back.

The choice was made for her. She heard a male voice shouting from the the stairwell. She couldn't make out what it was saying, but she didn't need to. 'Keep walking,' she hissed at Hwan. 'Act normal.'

But there was nothing normal about this situation: a terrified North Korean guide leading a teenage Chinese girl towards the hotel's exit. It was obvious to everybody that something was up. From the corner of her eye, Lili could see the receptionists talking and pointing. And they were barely halfway to the exit when the male voice shouted directly at them. Lili looked over her shoulder. A uniformed secret police officer had entered the reception area from the stairwell. He was screaming at them to stop.

Hwan *did* stop. But not for long. Lili revealed her pistol. She waved it in the direction of the police officer, who immediately hit the ground. The receptionists ducked down behind their desks.

'Run!' Lili screamed at Hwan, aiming the pistol at him. She knew the police officer would also be armed. She knew they only had seconds to get out of there. Their feet clattered across the hard floor of the hotel reception. Lili was faster than Hwan, and had to pull him along by the arm to get him to the exit. When they reached the glass door, the police officer was shouting again, but it wasn't clear who he was shouting at. He was still lying on the floor, but he had managed to access his pistol. He was stretching out his arm, pointing it at them.

Lili yanked the glass door open, pushed Hwan outside and followed. Just in time. A shot rang out from inside and a bullet slammed into the glass. It didn't shatter, but a spiderweb fracture spread out from the impact point with an icy crackle.

The flashing lights came from two police cars parked to

their left. Lili could see the silhouettes of drivers behind the wheels, and a passenger in each car. But there were no personnel outside the vehicles. It gave them a moment of opportunity. 'Run to the right,' she hissed at Hwan, brandishing the pistol in his direction. Hwan did as he was told. They sprinted along in front of the hotel, then across the street towards a line of trees that gave them a little cover. Lili's mind worked fast. They were on an island in the middle of the river. She did not doubt that the Pyongyang authorities could have it sealed off within minutes. If that happened, they would be trapped.

She had seen, when they drove to the hotel, that there were two bridges cutting across the island from the north of the city to the south. One bridge was for road vehicles. The other was for trains. They were sprinting along the north of the island, amid trees that grew between a main road on their left and the river on their right. They had to use one of these bridges to cross into the main part of Pyongyang, where they could try to lose themselves. And from this position, their quickest option was to head north.

Lili was a lot fitter than Hwan, who was out of breath after two minutes of running. She couldn't let him slow them down. Each time he lost pace, she pulled him by the arm or waved the pistol in his direction. His eyes were wild, and they grew wilder when they heard sirens. They seemed to be coming from all around. From behind, in the direction of the hotel. In the distance, from the south of the island. And to their right, on the opposite bank of the river, heading towards the bridge. Reinforcements were coming.

Lili forced them to up their pace, silently thanking the Watchers for putting them through such a brutal fitness regime over the past couple of months. The road bridge appeared ahead of them. It was broad and there was very little traffic. But on the other bank of the river, moving parallel to Lili and Hwan, were five – no, six – police cars, lights flashing, sirens sounding. They turned on to the bridge just as Lili and Hwan hit the road leading off it. To her left she could see sets of bright headlights coming from the other direction. They were cut off on both sides.

What to do? The police officer at the hotel must have raised the alarm and now he had reinforcements searching for them. She had to make a decision. Fast.

'Cross the road!' she screamed at Hwan. Before waiting for a reply, she hustled him across the highway as police vehicles closed in on them from both directions. They crossed in a matter of seconds, unsure if they had been spotted by the approaching vehicles. Lili had no time to worry about that. Straight ahead of them was the railway line. It was protected by a wire fence about four metres high.

'Climb it!' she screamed at Hwan.

Hwan was doubled up, trying to catch his breath, but he moved as Lili poked the gun into his ribs. He scaled the fence with difficulty, arms and legs sliding all over the wire mesh. Lili had to push him up from below as he struggled to reach the top. When he fell heavily on the other side, she was worried that he'd hurt himself. Lili climbed it more expertly, landing like a cat, and just in time. The police cars had crossed the bridge and were almost alongside them. Lili pressed Hwan to the ground, out of sight, just by the rail track. Her companion was shaking hard, from fear, exhaustion or both. The ground was a mixture of grit and soil, and he had his face pressed into it. Lili wasn't sure, but she thought he might be crying.

There was a new noise. It was faint, and drowned out by the sirens at first. But it quickly grew louder. A mechanical noise. Lili looked north. Nothing. She looked south and she saw them: the bright lights of a train thundering in their direction. Her stomach twisted in panic. She couldn't tell how far away the train was, but it was close and it was moving fast. They were lying right by the tracks. It was going to hit them . . .

'*Hwan! Move!*' she shouted. But Hwan didn't seem to know what was going on. She got to her knees and hauled him away from the track, back against the fence. They pressed themselves into the ground again. The noise of the train was deafening. It had almost reached them, and all Lili could do was hope they were out of its path.

The train missed them by a whisker. The noise was so loud it seemed to come from inside Lili's body. The air displacement blew her hair wildly. It took less than ten seconds to pass, but those ten seconds felt like ten minutes. Once it had passed, she felt more breathless than she had been after running from the hotel. Her face was blasted with grit and her ears were ringing. Hwan was still shaking. They remained pressed down into the ground for a full two minutes before Lili dared turn and look to her right.

Through the fence, she could make out activity on the bridge. Several vehicles had stopped halfway across it. In the beam of their headlights, she could make out the silhouettes of personnel moving in front of them. The police had set up a roadblock to stop anyone leaving the island.

But their attention was not focused on the railway bridge. They had made it over the fence unseen. Lili did not dare stand up for fear of revealing herself. She crawled so she was lying next to Hwan. 'What will happen if they catch us?' she demanded.

Hwan could barely speak for fear. It took several goes for him to answer. 'They will send us away,' he whispered. 'To a prison camp. For many years. Maybe for ever.'

'Do you want that to happen?'

'Of course not.'

'Then you'd better do exactly what I tell you. We can't stay here. They'll find us eventually. We need to get off the island. That means crawling along this rail track. You go first. Don't think of standing up and running. The guys at the roadblock will have weapons and they can shoot us at this distance. Do you understand?'

'Yes. But what happens when we get across the river?'

'When we get across the river, you and I are going to have a little talk. Then we're going to work out how to rescue my friends.' She checked the time: 01:30 hours. It had been a full forty-five minutes since Max and Lukas had been captured. The thought made her feel sick.

'Get moving,' she hissed. 'They're going to search this island thoroughly. We can't be here when they do.'

13

Prospero

The pain was all-consuming.

Max's abdomen was so bruised it hurt to breathe. He winced as he inhaled. His throat was sandpaper-dry. His lips were caked with dried blood from his nose. His head throbbed. It made it hard to think. Where was he? What had happened?

It all came back to him in a matter of seconds and he suddenly felt like retching again.

It was more than dark. There was no difference between eyes open and eyes closed. Thick, impenetrable blackness. All he knew was that he was lying on his front. The floor was hard and cold. Slightly damp. He was still wearing his wetsuit, which was clammy and tight, but the rebreathing apparatus and wrist unit had been taken from him. So too had the pistol and the chain cutters. Somewhere in the distance was the grinding hum of an engine. Slowly, painfully, Max pushed himself to a kneeling position. He felt nauseous and struggled to stay upright. Somehow he managed it.

His fists were clenched and sweating. He opened them up and prepared to feel around in the darkness, then remembered something Woody had told him in training. *If you don't know what you're about to touch, use the back of your hands, not your palms. It's less debilitating if you get burnt or cut.* He turned his hands so the backs were facing out, then pushed tentatively into the darkness.

Nothing.

He shuffled along on his knees. Only then did he feel something attached to his right ankle. It was uncomfortable, and when he moved, it dug painfully into his skin. He stretched out to feel what it was: a thick metal ring with what felt like an interlocking metal chain leading from it. He followed the chain with his fingertips. It was attached to a nearby wall. Max realised he was manacled.

'Is that you, Max?'

Max started, then felt a wave of relief as he recognised Lukas's voice. His friend sounded as bad as Max felt. His voice was weak and croaky. Max estimated that he was about three metres away, but he had no way of being sure.

'Mate,' Max whispered, 'what happened?'

'They knew we were coming,' Lukas said darkly. 'Someone tipped them off.'

There was a silence before they said, at the same time, 'Hwan.'

'I thought he was okay,' Max said.

'Me too,' Lukas admitted. 'I guess Hector was right when he said we shouldn't trust anybody.'

They remained silent for a minute.

'Are you chained up?' Max said.

'Yeah. We're not going anywhere by ourselves.'

'What do you think they're going to do with us?'

Another silence. Then Lukas said, 'I don't think they're going to kill us. I think they're going to torture us to find out who we are.'

It was then that they heard a third voice. Female. Throaty. The voice of a thousand cigarettes.

'What is this? The school playground?'

Max and Lukas said nothing. Max felt himself tensing up, ready to fight if he needed to.

'You're half right and half wrong of course,' the voice continued. 'They *are* going to torture you to find out who you are. You sound like youngsters, and they will be very interested to know more about you. But then they will kill you, and some innocent explanation will be found for your deaths. The world cannot know that the Korean regime is willing to eliminate young people as well as old.'

Max swallowed hard. 'Who are you?' he said.

'I was about to ask you the same thing.'

'Do you know anything about Prospero?' Lukas said.

'I've always hated that codename,' said the woman.

'Are *you* Prospero?' Max asked.

'Obviously.'

'But . . . you're a woman?'

'Last time I looked.'

'I thought . . .'

'You presumed. There's a big difference between presuming and thinking. Now tell me what you're doing here.'

'We're here to rescue you,' Max said.

There was a pause. Then a muffled sound which, after a few seconds, Max realised was laughter. Despite everything, he felt himself blushing in the darkness.

'What?' he said. 'What's so funny?'

'How would you say it's going, this grand rescue?' Prospero said. 'I expected help of some sort but – forgive me – not this. I suppose I have just learned something about how highly I am valued by my paymasters. Which is to say, not highly at all.'

'That's not true,' Lukas said. He sounded aggressive. Max could picture him jutting out his chin. 'There's five of us, and the others will be working something out. You'd better get ready.'

'Lukas . . .' Max hissed. He was giving away too much information. What if somebody was listening?

'Relax,' Prospero said. 'I am quite certain there are no English speakers on the boat. They are waiting for an English-speaking interrogator to arrive in the morning. I can't say I'm looking forward to making his – or her – acquaintance. But for now, we can speak freely.' She started to cough – a deeply unhealthy, chesty sound. When she'd recovered, she said, 'I have some matches in my shoe that they have failed to find. I'm going to light one so I can see your faces.'

There was a scratching sound, then a yellow flame illuminated the blackness. It was tiny, but enough to hurt Max's eyes. He only caught the briefest glimpse of Prospero's face, and of their surroundings.

The British spy was older than Max had imagined. Her

face was leathery and lined. It was also bruised, swollen and cut. One eye was barely open. Her upper lip was thick. She had clearly been badly beaten, and recently. She wore canvas trousers and a T-shirt, and was lean and muscular.

They were in a long space with steeply inclining metal walls dotted with painted metal rivets. Prospero was at one end. Max was three metres from her, Lukas the same distance from Max. The brief glimpse of their surroundings confirmed what Max already suspected: they were in the hull of the prison boat. And he clearly saw that they were each manacled to the boat's hull with a thick, short chain.

The light died, leaving a ghost of the flame on Max's retina. 'You're even younger than I expected,' Prospero said. She was unable to hide her disappointment.

'And you're even older,' Max said.

Prospero chuckled. 'Touché,' she said. 'Now tell me about this escape plan of yours.'

Max explained what they had tried to do. The swim upriver. The underwater welding kit. Their instruction to scuttle the boat and provide Prospero with a handgun so she could make her own escape from Pyongyang. 'Well,' the woman said when he'd finished, 'I can safely say I'm glad you failed.'

'What do you mean?' Lukas said. 'You don't want to get away?'

'Of course I want to get away. But you may have noticed that we are chained to the hull of this boat. If you had managed to scuttle it, there is no way I would have been able to escape. Of course, a more cynical person than

117

myself might jump to the conclusion that this was the whole point.'

'What do you mean?' Max said.

'I mean that if I *had* managed to escape, all well and good. But if I hadn't? I have many secrets that British intelligence would not want to fall into the hands of the North Korean authorities. If I were to die in the rescue attempt, that would be an acceptable outcome. Maybe even the best outcome.' She said this in a chilling, matter-of-fact manner, as if she expected and almost welcomed such an outcome. 'You've been sent on an assassination mission, my young friends, even though you didn't know it.'

'That's not true,' Max said hotly. 'We're here to rescue you. Our handlers were clear about that.'

'Rule number one of secret work,' Prospero said, 'accept that your handlers aren't telling you everything. Or that their superiors are keeping them in the dark. Somebody is always lying to somebody else. It's in our nature.'

'They'd have told us,' Max insisted. 'If our job was to kill you, they'd have said so.'

'And would you have done it?' Prospero asked.

Max had no answer for that.

'You're young,' Prospero said. 'And new to this. Perhaps you haven't yet stopped to ask yourself the question that we all ask ourselves, at some time or another.'

'What's that?'

'Why?' Prospero said. 'Why do we do what we do? We receive no praise. Nobody ever even hears about us, and we'll certainly never be rich. So why do we do it?' There was a long silence, then she said, 'The answer is simple of course.'

'What?' Lukas demanded.

'We do it,' Prospero said, 'because it's the right thing to do.'

'The way you're talking,' Lukas said, 'you think the right thing to do is to give up and let yourself die.' He sounded almost spiteful.

'I've been in this game for a long time, young man. You learn not to worry about what you can't control. During the Second World War, spies were routinely provided with cyanide pills for if they were captured. Sometimes a quick way out is better than the alternative. Choosing to die is not always the same as giving up, you know.'

'Wait,' Max said. An icy sensation was running through his blood. He remembered standing at the edge of the lake near Valley House, discussing whether they had acted the way the Watchers had intended. Sami had used exactly the same words as Prospero. *It was the right thing to do.* 'Lukas, if you were Abby and Sami, what would you be doing now?'

A beat. Then Lukas swore under his breath.

'Who are Abby and Sami?' Prospero said.

'Our friends,' said Max. 'They were in the river with us with a separate welding unit. If we activated our panic buttons, they were to return to the hotel, but . . .'

'But what?' Prospero said.

'If it was me,' said Lukas, 'and my friends had been caught, I would go after them.'

'The right thing to do,' Max muttered.

Prospero chuckled softly.

'Will you stop laughing?' Max said testily.

'I'm afraid that's unlikely to happen, boys,' Prospero said. 'While you were out cold, the barge moved position. We've travelled a good distance downstream. I'd say it's very unlikely they'll be able to get anywhere close to us.' She paused. 'Even if one of them is a girl,' she added quietly.

'You're wrong,' Max said. 'They'll find a way. Trust me. They're coming.'

A pause.

'In that case, my young friend, you need to prepare yourself.'

'For what?'

'I'd have thought that was obvious. For the end. If this barge sinks, we die. Your friends are also your cyanide capsules.'

Max was unable to suppress his anger. 'You want to give up now?' he said. 'Fine. *We're* not going to.' He tugged hard at the chain, several times. The only effect it had was to make his leg hurt.

'I'm not doubting your courage, young man. But if you work out a way to breathe underwater, be sure to let me know, won't you?'

Lukas swore again. Max tugged once more at the chain. Prospero fell silent.

Abby and Sami swam relentlessly. Within minutes they had reached the pier to which the prison boat had been moored.

The metal legs supporting it in the water were slimy and covered in algae. The cadets surfaced carefully underneath it. Hidden by the pier, they were able to check the activity on the river. It was still considerable. Five vessels had searchlights scanning the water. On the pier above them, they could hear footsteps and shouted instructions. But of the prison barge itself, there was no sign.

'We're low in the water,' Abby reminded them. 'We can't see far.'

Sami was grateful to her for not stating the obvious: that they had no idea how far the prison barge would travel, or if it would even be possible to catch up with it.

They didn't stay above the surface for long. The inky water was still sapping the warmth from them. The only way to stop their muscles seizing up was to keep moving. And that, of course, was also the only way to rescue Max and Lukas . . .

They submerged again and continued to follow the line of the river. Sami felt his fitness was starting to let him down. It was becoming difficult to instruct his limbs to do what he wanted. He sensed that Abby was having the same problem. When, after fifteen minutes, they almost swam straight into the hull of a small boat moored to the bank, it was a relief. It meant they had reached their first destination.

They broke the surface again gingerly, keeping in the shadow of the high bank. There was no activity in this part of the river. The search boats were all scouring the area where Max and Lukas had been captured. Here, all was silent, apart from the gentle clunking of the wooden boats knocking together.

Abby and Sami swam underneath them to reach the furthest boat. It was a rickety old thing, with a wooden hull and chipped paint. It had an outboard motor that stank of fuel. It made Sami nervous. He expected to have to use his welding gear to cut through the chain tying the boat to the bank. Then he saw that it wasn't a chain, but a rope knotted to a mooring ring. It took him and Abby a full five minutes to undo the tight, wet rope with their cold hands. The boat yawed precariously as they clambered in. It was particularly difficult for Sami with the welding gear strapped to his chest.

Abby checked the sat phone. There was still no signal, so they could contact neither Lili nor the Watchers. She turned her attention to the outboard motor.

'Please let the motor work,' Sami said fervently as Abby pulled the starting cord.

There was a feeble cough from the motor. It whimpered into nothing.

She pulled again. Even less.

'We're going to have to swim it,' Sami said. Even he was aware that his voice sounded weak.

Abby, however, had an expression of intense concentration on her face. She gave the starting cord a third, violent tug. The motor spluttered into life. Within seconds they were moving.

The cadets crouched low in the boat, Sami at the stern, Abby steering them at the helm, shivering in the night air.

They kept to the shadows, close to the bank. Continuing downstream, they were soon completely out of sight of the search boats as they scanned the water up ahead for the prison barge.

14

A Bag of Rice

It was slow work for Lili and Hwan, crawling along the railway bridge to the mainland of Pyongyang. But it was better to be slow than to be caught.

Lili's knees and elbows were sore and scraped, her throat and lungs full of thick, choking dust. Every thirty seconds she had to hiss at Hwan to keep moving. Her Korean captive was a mess. He kept collapsing. Lili couldn't tell if it was through fear or lack of fitness. Eventually, however, they reached the far side of the railway bridge. Lili could still see the flashing lights of the roadblock on the road bridge. She shuddered to think what would happen if they were caught.

Time check: 02:00 hours. She thought of Max and Lukas and what must have happened to them. Her anger at Hwan redoubled. 'Hey,' she hissed. 'Stop here.'

Hwan seemed pleased to obey. From his crawling position he collapsed and lay face down. Lili raised her binoculars and scanned the darkness. She could see a train station up ahead. To their left, trees. To their right, open ground, but deserted. They would need to climb the fence again to reach either. For now, they were alone and unseen. This would be a good place to talk.

'Sit up,' she told Hwan. 'Do it!'

Hwan pushed himself up miserably from his prone position. He sat next to Lili, who had her back to the railway fence, and hugged his knees. Lili removed her sat phone, switched it on and checked the signal. It was good. She could make a call to the Watchers. But to brief them properly, she needed to know what information Hwan had given the North Korean authorities.

'You reported us,' Lili said. It was a statement, not a question. Hwan did not deny it. 'Who did you call?'

Hwan stared blankly across the track. 'I am your chaperone,' he said. 'All chaperones have a member of the secret police they must call if they suspect anything strange.'

'And why did you suspect us?'

'Because I saw you and the other two outside the fifth floor. One of your friends, Lukas – he was wearing the shoes that divers wear. That's all I told my secret police contact.'

Lili shook her head. 'I don't get it, Hwan,' she said. 'I thought we all got on okay. You could have just kept quiet.'

Hwan made a cynical, dismissive sound. 'You do not understand,' he said.

'Then *make* me understand. My friends are in danger. I'll do anything to help them. Right now, none of my ideas end too well for you. So seriously, make me understand.'

'I was in trouble! First when those officers scolded me outside the Tower of the Juche Ideology because your friend was being disrespectful. Then when I was seen accepting food from Max. These things are not allowed.'

'And you were afraid you were going to be punished?'

Hwan rolled his eyes, as if that were a ridiculous suggestion. 'No,' he said quietly. 'I was not worried that *I* would be punished.'

'Then . . .'

'You've heard of the camps?' Hwan said.

'The concentration camps? Yes.'

'We are not supposed to know about them. The authorities deny that they exist. But we do know about them. They do exist. Countless people have been sent to these camps for the smallest offences.' He paused. 'Including my parents.'

He glanced down. Suddenly Lili didn't know what to say. All she managed was, 'Why?'

'Because that is what happens in my country.'

'What did they do?'

'My father stole a bag of rice. We were starving and we had no money.' He hesitated. 'Do you know what it is like to be starving?'

Lili shook her head.

'You will eat anything. Grass. Weeds. Shoes. But it's not proper food and your body knows it. You waste away. Your eyeballs look as if they are bulging from their sockets. It's just your face growing thin, but that is what it looks like. People fight over the smallest scraps of food. They kill for it. It's that, or die of starvation. My father stole the rice without hesitation. There was nothing else he could do. But he was caught.' Hwan paused. 'He and my mother were sentenced to death.'

Lili stared at him. 'For a bag of rice?'

'In my country, people are killed for smaller crimes than

that. Especially if they are the wrong *songbun*.'

'So . . .'

'They were to be executed in public,' Hwan continued. 'This was four years ago, when I was still at school. The execution was to take place in the school grounds.'

'What?' Lili whispered.

'It is normal,' Hwan said. 'Children from the age of seven are forced to watch public executions, so they understand what happens if they do bad things. I was to watch my parents die, along with all my friends.'

Lili didn't know what to say. She suddenly felt very cold.

'My uncle – my father's brother – is a major in the Korean People's Army. The day before my parents were to be executed, I travelled to his house in Pyongyang. He was not pleased to see me. I begged him to do something, to speak to someone. He sent me away, told me never to return to his house. I understood. He did not want his family to be in danger because of me. But perhaps he did something. Perhaps he bribed the right person. Because the next day it was announced that my parents would not be executed after all. Instead they would be sent to a hard labour camp. They disappeared. I have not seen them since.'

'Are they still . . . ?'

'Alive? I do not know. But I think perhaps they are. Six months ago, a neighbour returned from the prison camp. It is very unusual that this happens. But he did, and he told me my parents were still there. Very frail. But alive.' He gave Lili an intense stare. 'You asked me if I was afraid of being punished. No. I am not afraid for myself. I am afraid for my mother and father. If I do something wrong, there is a chance that *they* will be punished.' He swallowed hard. 'And if I do something right . . .'

'There's a chance that they will be released,' Lili said.

Hwan nodded.

'That's why you did it,' Lili said quietly. 'That's why you told your contact that you had seen us on the fifth floor. Because informing on us means rewards for you. It means your parents might be released.'

He nodded again. 'But now,' he said, 'there is no hope. They will say I helped you escape.'

'No,' Lili said. 'I had you at gunpoint!'

Hwan gave a cynical laugh. 'You think they will care about that?'

'What were you supposed to do when I was waving a pistol in your face?'

'That's easy,' said Hwan. 'I was supposed to die. For the party and the motherland. Now, if I'm lucky, they will send me to a prison camp. And if I'm unlucky . . .' He didn't finish the sentence.

Lili was enraged. Her blood burned with injustice. And with shame. She had misunderstood Hwan. Misunderstood his motives. Misunderstood everything about him. She stared at the satellite phone in her hand. Her duty was clear. Her friends were in danger. She had to do everything possible to rescue them. That meant making contact with the Watchers – and she knew what their instruction would be. *Trust nobody.* Especially Hwan. He had betrayed them once. Given the opportunity, he would betray them again.

What would they instruct Lili to do? Tie him up here by the railway track? Worse? Would they make her punish this young North Korean man for no crime other than trying to save his own parents?

Not if Lili had her way. A determined expression crossed her face.

'We're going to get them out,' she said.

Hwan blinked at her. 'What?'

'Your mum and dad. We're going to get them out of that prison camp.'

'What are you talking about?' Hwan said. 'It is hundreds of miles away. I don't even know the exact location.'

'It doesn't matter,' she said. 'I've got a plan. But we need to work together, Hwan. And we need to trust each other. Can we manage that, do you think?'

'How can I trust you?' Hwan said. 'I don't even know who you are. You are not ordinary tourists. I knew that from the moment I saw you. But why are the secret police chasing you? What are you doing here?'

Trust nobody. The words echoed in Lili's mind. But if she was asking Hwan to trust her, she had to trust him in return. 'There is a British agent being held prisoner in a boat on the river. We're here to rescue him.'

'But you are just . . . just children.'

'Go figure,' Lili muttered. 'I think Max and Lukas have been caught. I don't know what's happened to Abby and Sami. But I do know this: I'm going to do everything necessary to get them to safety. And you're in luck, because my plan includes getting your mum and dad to safety too.'

'It's too dangerous,' Hwan whispered.

'Sure, it's dangerous. It's also the only chance they have. Hwan, if my plan works, I'll be reunited with my friends and you'll be reunited with your parents. When you think about the alternative, are you telling me that's not worth a try?' She held out her hand. Hwan stared at it. Then he took Lili's hand in his, and they shook.

'What do you want me to do?' he asked quietly.

'First things first,' said Lili. She held up the sat phone and started dialling an access code. 'I've got a call to make,' she said.

There was enough fuel in Abi and Sami's outboard motor to propel them a good distance downstream, past another island in the river and into the unpopulated waters beyond. Then it spluttered and died. But that was okay, because they could see the prison barge.

It was anchored in the middle of the river. There were lights on board, but not many, and no searchlights. No other vessels surrounded it. It was alone and out of the way.

Here, further from the centre of Pyongyang, the river bank was not so high. They were able to exit their boat and drag it on to a narrow stretch of sludgy shingle which led to a tree-lined area. They were shivering with cold. The prospect of entering the water again was not inviting.

'Do you think Max and Lukas are still alive?' Abby asked quietly as they crouched by the boat.

'I am certain of it,' Sami said fiercely. He did not admit that he had been wondering the same thing. 'And we are going to rescue them. Check your sat phone. Maybe you can get a signal now.'

Abby pulled out her handset and powered it up. 'Bingo,' she said. 'Who do I call? Lili or the Watchers?'

'The Watchers,' Sami said firmly. 'And quickly.'

But Abby was already dialling, keying in her access code with a stiff, trembling index finger. Once she had entered it, she put the sat phone to her ear.

A voice answered almost immediately.

15

The New Deal

The operations room was a small concrete building two miles from the border between North Korea and South Korea. On its roof was a communications satellite dish. Nearby was a helicopter landing zone. Inside the ops room were a number of glowing laptops, cables snaking across the floor, a digital clock on the wall showing the local time and GMT, detailed maps of Pyongyang and North Korea in general, and five people. Two were South Korean military personnel. The other three were British.

Hector, Woody and Angel sat at separate laptops. They wore earpieces and boom mics. Since arriving here from Beijing they had been in constant communication with the military authorities in charge of South Korean airspace. And with a Royal Navy frigate patrolling the waters off the west coast of the Korean peninsula. And with their faceless superiors in Whitehall.

But above all, they were waiting for a call from the Special Forces Cadets. A call to tell them the operation had been a success, that the prison ship had been scuppered and the cadets were safely back in their hotel rooms.

They knew, when two calls came in at the same time from

separate sat phones, that this was not what had happened. They exchanged anxious glances and checked the clock: 02:15 hours. Hector tapped his keyboard to accept both calls and patch them in to a three-way conversation.

'Go ahead,' he said curtly.

The Watchers heard two voices at the same time. Abby and Lili talked maniacally over each other, clearly panicked.

'Quiet,' Hector barked. And when they fell silent, 'Abby, you first.'

– *They've got Max and Lukas! They were waiting for us! They knew we were coming!*

Woody swore. Angel pinched the bridge of her noise.

'Where are they now?' Hector said.

– *On the barge, we think.*

'What is your current position?'

– *We're on the northern river bank. The barge moved downriver and we followed it. We still have one underwater welding kit. We're preparing to make our approach and scuttle the barge.*

'Keep your position for now.'

– *But what if Max and Sami are—*

'Keep your position! Lili, go ahead.'

The Watchers listened intently as Lili explained the events of the last hour. The escape from the hotel. The blockade on the bridge. The railway track. Hwan. As she started to explain about Hwan's parents and the prison camp, Hector interrupted.

'I'm sorry for the guy,' he said, 'but you're not there to right every injustice you come across. Our priority is to get Max and Lukas out of there safely. Our next priority is Prospero. I'm afraid Hwan and his parents don't come into it.'

– *Yes, they do. You have to hear me out, Hector. I'm not going to let this go.*

Angel made a 'let her speak' gesture.

'Go ahead . . .' Hector said carefully.

– *Don't you see? Hwan is our best chance. The North Koreans don't know where Abby and Sami are. We need to get Hwan to call his secret police contact and say that he's been kidnapped by me, Abby and Sami – the three of us – and we're taking him to a pick-up location on the northern edge of Pyongyang. They'll send their forces to that location and wait for us to turn up. Only we won't be coming. Hwan and I will make our way to the real pick-up location – you said it was a deserted football stadium, right? – while Abby and Sami rescue Max, Lukas and Prospero. We all rendezvous at the football stadium and meet the stealth chopper there. Then we get out of here.*

'I don't like it,' Hector said immediately. 'How do we know we can trust Hwan to deliver the correct message to the secret police? How do we know the authorities will believe him?'

– *We can* trust him, *and he'll be very convincing. Because when we've made it out of the country with Prospero, we offer the North Koreans a new deal. Their two spies in return for releasing Hwan's parents, and letting Jerry and Elsa leave the country.*

There was a heavy silence in the ops room.

'Hold the line,' Hector said. He muted the conversation and turned to Woody and Angel. The faces of all three Watchers were etched with concern.

'She makes it sound easy,' Angel said. There was a note of pride in her voice.

'Too easy,' Hector said. 'A plan like that doesn't just happen. It takes hours of planning. Days, even. Contingencies. Backup strategies.'

'Do we have a better idea?' Woody said tersely. 'We just call the North Koreans, 'fess up and ask for our child spies back?'

'They'd have a better chance of survival that way.'

'You're letting your relationship with Max cloud your thinking, Hector,' Angel said.

'That's not true.'

'If we hand those kids over to the North Koreans, they could be in prison – or worse – for the next twenty years.'

'At least they'd still be alive,' Hector said.

'But would they want to be?' Woody demanded. 'Face it, Hector. That's not an option. The way I see it, our choices are pretty limited. The cadets are scattered all around Pyongyang. Two of them are already incarcerated. They've no chance of getting to the emergency pick-up zone without help. Maybe this Hwan guy is the answer. People will do an awful lot to stop their families getting hurt.'

'We don't even know if his parents are still alive,' Hector said.

'It doesn't matter,' said Woody. 'It's the chance of seeing his mum and dad again that makes Hwan trustworthy.'

'Too many things can go wrong,' Hector countered. 'A plan like that sounds okay when you say it. Actually *doing* it is a different matter.'

'You've forgotten what it's like to be young, Hector,' Angel said. 'It's much easier to do things when you don't know they're impossible. That's why the Special Forces Cadets are so valuable. You and I would think twice about a strategy like this. Those kids? They might just pull it off.'

'Remember the lake,' Woody said. 'They worked together like a real team. And they were too strong for us. They've got the makings of a good unit, Hector. We need to give them the chance to prove themselves. And let's face it, Lili's suggestion is a classic military strategy: get the enemy looking in one direction while the interesting stuff is happening somewhere else.'

Hector bowed his head. He inhaled deeply, then he connected to the call again. 'Tell Hwan we'll offer his government the new deal as soon as you're out of the country. And tell him that if we suspect him of double-crossing us at any point, the deal is off.'

– *He won't double-cross us. Trust me.*

'I don't trust anyone,' Hector said. 'You'd be wise to do the same. RV at the emergency pick-up point at 04:00 hours.'

– *That's not enough time . . .*

'It's the best we can do. The chopper has to return during the hours of darkness. Sunrise is at 06:00. If we leave it any later, we'll be seen. RV at 04:00, not a second later. Is that understood?'

– *Understood*, said Lili.

– *Understood*, said Abby.

The line went dead. Hector turned to the others. 'Get the stealth chopper prepared,' he said. 'I want it ready to go in two minutes. We're cutting it fine as it is. Warn the Foreign Office that we're about to breach North Korean airspace. And let's make sure we get something out of it.'

'Roger that,' Woody and Angel said in unison.

'Abby, can you still hear me? Abby?'

But nobody answered. If Lili wanted to speak to Abby again, she would have to dial her sat phone directly. She was about to do that when Hwan, who was watching Lili with an expression of great expectation, asked, 'What did they say?'

'They said okay.' Lili looked around. 'We need to get away from this railway track. Do you have a mobile phone?'

Hwan shook his head. 'They took it away from me.'

'Then we need a pay phone. Do they even have pay phones in Pyongyang?'

'A few,' Hwan said. 'We cannot use them to call outside the country.'

'We don't need to. Where is the nearest one?'

Hwan pointed along the line towards the train station.

Lili shook her head. 'It's too public. Where else?'

Hwan thought for a moment. 'I think there is one in a street near Taedong Bridge. There will not be many people there at this time of night.'

'Okay,' Lili said. 'That's where we'll go. When we get there, you're going to call your secret police contact. The one you told about us. Can you do that?'

Hwan nodded.

'You tell him you've been abducted by me, Abby and Sami. By the three of us – that's really important. Do you understand that?'

'But they will not believe that you have allowed me to make a phone call.'

'I'll explain how we get round that in a minute. First I have to speak to Abby.' She was about to dial the number when they heard voices. Shouts. She raised her binoculars and looked south along the railway line, back the way they'd come. She was dazzled by flashes of torchlight. People were on the track, searching for something. No prizes for guessing what. She thought she heard a dog barking.

Lili's heart felt like it might stop.

'Back over the fence!' she hissed. But Hwan was staring at the torchlight too, and he seemed unable to move. Lili shook him by the arm.

'Quickly! Hwan! *Quickly!*'

His attention snapped back. He looked at Lili in panic.

'I'll help you over again,' she whispered. 'But we have to do it now. That dog's getting closer – can't you hear it?'

He nodded, then faced the fence and grasped the links. Lili cupped her hands under his right foot and hoisted him up. Hwan scrambled inexpertly to the top of the fence then hauled himself over. This time he landed a little less heavily. He turned back to Lili, but his eyes widened and he pointed along the track. Lili saw what he was pointing at: two dogs, snarling, metres away and bolting in her direction.

She flung herself at the fence, arms stretched above her head. With a surge of adrenaline she pulled herself up, her arms straining to take her weight. Had she been half a second later, she would have been food for the dogs. As it was, they jumped, barked and snapped at her heels. A gasp escaped her as she struggled to pull herself up the fence, the wire cutting into the skin of her hands. She could hear the shouting getting louder and closer, but she didn't dare turn her head. She was concentrating on scaling the fence and could only look up to ensure her next handhold was good.

The fence was shaking and rattling. The dogs were in a frenzy, snarling and scratching at the wire. Lili summoned all her strength to swing her legs over the top of the fence. She landed right next to Hwan. Only then did she check over her shoulder. She couldn't see the people holding the torches because they were behind the light. But she could tell they were running towards her – and quickly. She jumped to her feet, pulled Hwan to his, and sprinted towards a clump of trees. Hidden among the thick trunks, her lungs burning, she turned to look back at the railway line.

The dogs were dancing and circling, still barking ferociously. They obviously had Lili and Hwan's scent. Four or five men were shouting at them to be quiet and shining their torches through the railway fence towards the trees. Had they seen Lili and Hwan? Did they intend to follow?

Then she saw a couple of the torches pointing at the other side of the railway, as if their pursuers weren't sure which way their quarry had escaped.

'Did they see us?' Hwan whispered.

'I don't know,' said Lili. 'Maybe. I think those dogs could follow our scent, if they had the chance. But they can't get them over the fence.'

'They could cut through,' said Hwan.

Lili nodded grimly. She checked the time. 02:30 hours. Her stomach turned to ice. They only had an hour and a half to get to the pick-up zone.

'How far is the payphone?' she asked.

'From here, about ten minutes. We have to go under the bridge and along the river. But we mustn't run. If anybody sees us, they will know we are trying to escape from something. And then . . .' He was clearly terrified at the prospect of what might happen.

'Lead the way,' Lili said. 'And Hwan, remember, if this works you see your mum and dad very soon. But if it doesn't . . .'

Hwan swallowed hard, nodded, and started to move through the trees towards the main road that ran alongside the river. Lili followed, clutching her sat phone in her sweaty hand. She had to a call to make, and she had to make it now.

16

The Call

'We need to go. We only have an hour and a half. Come on! We need to go!' Sami seemed desperate to re-enter the water. Abby agreed. Max and Lukas were only fifty metres away. A short swim, compared to what they'd already done. All Abby could think about was cutting through the hull of the boat to rescue them.

But something held her back. Sami was always quick to act. Sometimes *too* quick. Sometimes his emotions trumped everything else. It was a boy thing, she had often thought. Abby knew that sometimes there was time to stop and think. Now was one of those times. She was not moving to the water's edge quite so quickly.

'It's going to be difficult to get to the pick-up zone, the old football stadium,' she said. 'We don't know our way there, and as soon as the ship is scuttled, the place will be crawling with police and military . . .'

'We can't worry about that now,' Sami said. He was ankle-deep in the river. 'Who knows what they're doing to Max and Lukas? They could be dead if we leave it any longer.'

'They could also be dead if we mess this up,' Abby replied.

'And the same goes for the rest of us. Just . . . just hold on a minute. Let me think this through.' And under her breath, she muttered, 'I wish Angel was here.'

As she spoke, her sat phone rang. She answered it immediately. 'Go ahead.'

– *It's me. Lili.* She sounded out of breath.

'Where are you?'

– *I'm with Hwan. We're making our way to a phone booth. Listen, you can't enter the water yet.*

'Try telling that to Sami.' He was knee-deep already.

– *Put me on speaker phone.*

Abby checked her surroundings. The river bank was deserted, but she wanted to be sure there was nobody around to overhear them. There was a line of trees just beyond the bank. She scanned it carefully for movement. There was nothing.

'Sami,' she hissed. 'Get back here, quickly.'

With obvious reluctance, Sami trudged back out of the water as she put the phone on speaker.

'Go ahead,' she said.

– *We haven't made the call yet.* Lili sounded like she was walking fast. *We might have been spotted. We might have dogs after us.*

'Sounds like it's going pretty well,' Abby said.

– *You can't sink the barge yet. We have to wait until we're sure the North Koreans believe Hwan's story.*

'How are we ever going to know that?' Abby asked.

– *There are police cars all over the place near the hotel. I'm sure they'll start heading north if they think that's where they're going to find us. We'll see them doing it. But if they don't believe Hwan, they'll realise it's a trick and that puts you in more danger. And if you sink the boat before we make the call, they'll know Hwan's lying. You've got to wait until I give you the go-ahead.*

Abby looked at Sami. He was clearly torn.

'She's right, Sami,' Abby said. 'We have to wait.'

Sami was almost crying. 'But what if they –'

'We *have* to. Lili, we're going to wait for your call. Make it quickly.'

There was no reply. The sat-phone screen faded as Lili hung up.

'Come on,' Abby said. 'We're too exposed here. Anyone can see us. Let's get behind the treeline.'

Sami glanced back at the barge. Then he nodded. 'It's dangerous, what she's doing,' he said.

'You know,' Abby replied, 'I've got a feeling we need to get used to that.'

Without another word, they gathered up their gear and headed for the trees.

Sweat ran uncomfortably down the nape of Lili's neck. Her back prickled, as though somebody was watching her. As she and Hwan hurried along the main road, she kept checking over her shoulder. All she saw was an empty pavement. No military or police uniforms. No dogs. Somehow it failed to put her mind at rest. Glancing up, she saw a security camera on a lamppost. It was pointing on to the road itself, but she wondered how many hidden cameras they had passed. If anybody saw video footage of her and Hwan hurrying away from the railway, her plan wouldn't work. But it would take time to review camera footage in detail. By then, they'd be gone.

The road took them along the north bank of the river. They were almost level with the hotel on its island. Across the water, Lili could still see the lights of police cars around the hotel. There was still activity there. It made her want to run, but Hwan had been right: running would be suspicious. So they kept close to the wall on the left of the pavement, where a shadow camouflaged them.

'How much further?' Lili whispered.

'Not far now,' Hwan said. He pointed ahead at another building. 'The Pyongyang Hotel,' he said. 'Tourists do not stay there. Only government officials. The phone booth is just past that.'

'Government officials?' Lili said weakly. There was activity outside this second hotel. Cars approaching and leaving, despite the time, but nobody seemed to be getting in and out of them. The streets were otherwise completely empty. Lili and Hwan stood breathlessly at a T-junction. They had to cross the road, but they risked being seen by the people in the cars outside the hotel. Lili checked her watch. 02:40 hours. There was so little time.

'We can't wait,' she said. 'We have to cross. Hold my hand. People will think we're a couple that way.'

Hwan agreed. His palm was wet and clammy, his grip weak. They looked straight ahead as they crossed the road, because staring at the vehicles outside this hotel would draw attention to themselves. When they reached the other side of the road, they unclasped their hands. Taedong Bridge was thirty metres ahead. The road led underneath the bridge, and they stopped there in the echoing darkness. Just beyond the bridge was a phone booth. They stared at it. Then Hwan turned to Lili.

'What do I say?' he asked.

Lili took a few seconds to get everything straight in her head. They might have been seen on the railway line, so she had to include that possible sighting in Hwan's story.

'Stick to the truth as closely as you can,' she said. She knew the best lies were the ones that contained an element of truth. 'Say I forced you out of the hotel at gunpoint. Say we escaped the island along the rail track. Tell them about the dogs. Tell them that Abby and Sami were waiting for us on the other side of the railway fence. That's really important, Hwan. The authorities can't know that Abby and Sami are preparing to rescue Max and Lukas. They need to think they're with us. Do you get that?'

Hwan nodded silently.

'Tell me a good place on the northern outskirts of Pyongyang where a helicopter could safely land to pick us up. It needs to be well out of the way of crowds and houses.'

Hwan made a helpless gesture. A gesture that said: what do I know of helicopters and landing zones?

'*Think*, Hwan. Your parents' lives depend on it.'

Hwan pinched his furrowed brow. 'The old rice fields,' he said. 'There is a disused warehouse with a concrete area in the front for vehicles. It is about two miles from the city centre. I'm sure nobody will be there now.'

'Good,' Lili said. 'You need to tell your secret police contact that we're heading there. Say we're taking you with us because we didn't trust you not to go straight to the authorities but we weren't brave enough to kill you.'

'*Are* you brave enough to kill me?' Hwan said.

Lili didn't answer. 'Tell them you managed to escape, and you ran straight to the nearest payphone to report what happened.'

'But . . .' Hwan was flustered, 'they will come and find me. And then they will torture me so I tell them the truth.'

'Are you a good actor, Hwan?'

'No,' he said.

'Well, tonight you'd better be. When you've given them that information, you suddenly need to sound frightened. Say you can see us, that we've found you, that we're running in your direction and we have a gun. Tell them to rescue you at the old rice fields. Then drop the phone and leave it hanging. They'll think we've abducted you again.'

Hwan stared at her. 'It will never work.'

'That all depends on how convincing you are,' Lili said. 'I know if it was *my* mum and dad . . .'

'Where *are* your parents?' Hwan said.

'They're dead,' Lili said quietly. 'Believe me, I'd do anything to get them back. And I know you would too.'

Hwan breathed deeply. 'You are harsh,' he said. 'But I think you are kind too.' He fished a coin from his pocket. 'I will do it.'

They peered out from under the bridge to check that they weren't being observed. Lili could just hear a police siren, but it wasn't close and they couldn't see anybody. They hurried over to the phone booth. Hwan picked up the receiver with a trembling hand. Lili scoured the area for threats while Hwan dialled a number and inserted the coin.

Lili spoke four languages. Korean was not one of them, but as a linguist she understood the tone and inflexion of somebody's voice, even without understanding the words they spoke. So it was with Hwan. As he started to speak, she could tell he sounded panicked and breathless. He jabbered, falling over his words as if he couldn't get them out quickly enough. He sounded convincingly scared.

Then he stopped. He whispered something. He nodded at Lili. She nodded back. Hwan dropped the phone. It clattered and swung by its cord. For the benefit of the person at the other end of the line, Lili grabbed Hwan and said, 'You come with us. Try to run again and I'll shoot you.' And she dragged him away from the phone.

Lili intended to get up on to Taedong Bridge and cross the river. That would put them on the correct bank to make their way to the real pick-up zone. But then something happened that almost made her heart fail. There was the sound of a police siren. It was coming from the north. As they ran to a stone staircase that led up to the bridge, they saw flashing neon lights. The police car had stopped on the northern bank of the bridge, metres from the phone booth.

A dreadful thought crossed her mind. Had the authorities been able to trace Hwan's call immediately and dispatch a police car to investigate? She hadn't even considered that this would be possible. All she knew was, they had to get away. Crossing the bridge was impossible: it was blocked. Going back the way they had come would be foolhardy. Heading north, in the direction Hwan had told his contact they would be fleeing, was obviously out. It left only one option: to follow the river.

But first, they needed to be sure their plan had worked.

'This way,' Lili hissed. They ran away from the bridge, past the phone booth where the handset was still swinging, towards a line of cars parked on the broad riverside road. It was the only cover she could see. Hardly ideal, but it would have to do. They crouched down between two vehicles – an old black saloon and a scuffed van with rusty panels. Hwan pressed his back to the bonnet of the van. He was sweating again, and muttering something to himself, over and over. Lili peered through the binoculars from between the two vehicles. She had a good view of Taedong Bridge, where the police car was still parked. And she could see the Yanggakdo Hotel on its island where they had been staying. She could just make out the lights and movements of the authorities still busying themselves around the hotel.

'What do we do now?' Hwan whispered.

Lili checked the time. 02:45 hours. 'Now,' she said, 'we watch.'

A minute passed.

Two minutes.

There was no change. Nothing happened. The police car remained on Taedong Bridge. The activity around the hotel continued. With each minute, Lili's stomach felt more leaden. Her strategy hadn't worked. There was no sign that the North Koreans had believed Hwan's story. Hector's reluctance to agree to the plan echoed in her mind. He had been right. She had been wrong.

Hwan was clearly having similar thoughts. 'I don't know if he believed me. He kept asking me questions.'

'What sort of questions?'

'How I escaped. How I knew where you were heading. I didn't have good answers . . .'

'Well, it's too late now,' Lili snapped. Anxiety gnawed at her. She even began to wonder if Hwan had said the right thing. Maybe he'd been tricking her all along.

She was on the point of turning to her companion to confront him when she heard the helicopter. It came as if from nowhere, appearing from the south, fierce searchlights burning down into Pyongyang. The lights even lit up their hiding place, but only for a fraction of a second as the helicopter powered its way north.

And then there were the police cars. The one guarding the Taedong Bridge stayed in place, as three others screamed over the bridge from the far bank of the river. And by the hotel, there was a commotion. More police cars were heading towards the bridge that led off the island. Lili imagined seeing Pyongyang from a great height. She envisaged the vehicles like fireflies in the night, all heading north in the direction of their prey.

'What is it?' Hwan hissed. 'What is happening?'

But Lili didn't answer. She just lowered her binoculars,

pulled out her sat phone and dialled a number. Abby answered almost immediately.

– *Yeah?*

'They've fallen for it,' Lili said. 'They're on their way to the fake pick-up point. You can rescue Max, Lukas and Prospero. Do it. Now.'

17

Chai

02:50 hours. Sami didn't need telling twice.

He and Abby knew that Lili's plan was working even before she had called them. They had seen the first helicopter heading north, and now two more were going in the same direction. Sami strode from the treeline towards the water, rebreather and underwater welding unit still strapped to his body. He was ankle-deep again before he turned and urged Abby to join him. 'Quickly. We don't have time to waste.'

Abby hurried down to the water. They looked out at the barge. Its deck was deserted.

'We can't swim underwater,' Sami whispered. 'We have no way of navigating to the boat, and the current is strong. We have to keep our heads above water until we get there. We might be seen. It's risky.'

'Tell me which bit of this *isn't* risky,' Abby muttered. 'Listen, when the time comes, you need to cut a hole big enough for somebody to swim through. And it's quicker to do a circle than a square.'

Sami raised an eyebrow.

'Ah, so I used to pay attention in maths,' she said. 'The perimeter of a – oh, never mind, just cut a circle, okay?'

'Okay.' Without another word, they fitted their rebreathing masks and strode into the water. Within seconds they were shoulder-deep. Then they were swimming.

The water seemed colder than before, the current stronger. It was a struggle to keep on target. Sami could tell he had less energy than before. The night's work had taken its toll and it was an effort even to keep afloat. But he and Abby kept going, muscles and lungs burning, growing closer to the boat, bit by bit.

It was the silence that got to Max, even more than the darkness. The faint thrum of the engines had stopped and there were no voices. Apart from their own steady breathing and, a minute ago, the sound of helicopters somewhere in the distance, there was nothing. No sound to indicate what their captors had in mind for them, or whether anyone was coming to the rescue. Occasionally, half-heartedly, he would pull at the chain that fixed him to the hull of the boat. Each time he did it, Prospero chided him in her rough voice: 'Save your energy. You'll need it for whatever our captors have in mind.'

Each time, either Max or Lukas would say, 'Our friends are coming.'

And Prospero would say, 'I hope not, kids. It's a long way to the bottom of this river, and I can think of better ways to die.'

So could Max. Panic rose in his chest as he imagined the horror of being chained to the hull as the boat sank. He imagined shouting for help, and the moment when they couldn't shout any more because the hull was full of water . . .

He found himself holding his breath, imagining what it would be like.

Stay away, he thought. *Please stay away from the boat. You'll kill us all if you scupper it now . . .*

The boat was almost in touching distance. Its presence changed the current of the river and it was all Sami could do to stay afloat.

Abby was right next to him. It was clear she was also having difficulty, but together they finally reached the hull. It loomed threateningly above them. Close-up, it was much bigger than it had seemed from the shore. Sami uncomfortably imagined that huge block of metal and fuel sinking, with him trapped below it. The thought made him want to swim away. He had to muster all his courage.

He felt for the underwater welding kit strapped to his chest, then he looked at Abby. They nodded in unison. Then they pushed themselves below the surface.

Stay away, Max prayed. *Please stay away.* He tugged on the metal chain.

'Leave it –' Prospero started to say.

But Max interrupted. 'Just . . . just let me *think*,' he hissed. He could tell that Prospero had no faith that the cadets would come to their rescue. He had to work this one out for himself, but he couldn't get the thought of drowning out of his head.

That thought triggered something in his memory. He was back in first class on the flight to Beijing. Hector was explaining the plan for entering the river. When he had finished, Abby had spoken. What was it she'd said? *I'm not going to lie. I've always been terrified of drowning. I'm beginning to wish we'd spent more time learning to dive and less time on the old Morse code.*

And Hector had berated her. *Morse is an important skill.*

An important skill . . . and one in which all the cadets were thoroughly versed.

'We need to warn them that we're chained up,' Max said suddenly.

'How're we going to do that?' Lukas said. His voice had lost all patience. 'Instagram?'

'No,' Max said. 'Not Instagram. Like this.'

He clenched his fist and started to pound a rhythm against the hull. His thumping made a dull sound. He could only pray that it would be audible in the water.

A slimy metal ring protruded from the hull. Sami grabbed it. Then he turned his attention to the underwater welding unit, which he handled with great care. There was a thin metal lance attached to a handheld trigger mechanism. A narrow pipe led to the fuel canisters strapped to his chest. The weight of the gear kept him just below the surface of the water. He positioned the cutting lance so its end was almost touching the hull. Abby trod water next to him. He gave her a warning nod through the murky water, then prepared to ignite the welding unit.

A muffled thud stopped him.

He didn't know what it was. It was very quiet, hardly there at all. But it seemed to come from inside the hull of the boat. For a horrible moment, he thought it was the vessel's engines starting up again, but then there was another thud. Then a third and a fourth. The gaps between the four thuds had a distinct pattern. Long short long short. There was a pause before the thuds started again. Short short short short . . .

Sami understood immediately. It was a message, delivered in Morse code. The first two letters had been a C and an H. Short long. Short short. An A and an I.

C – H – A – I –

The thudding stopped. Sami repeated the letters in his head. Chai? That didn't make sense. Then the thudding started again.

N – E – D – U – P – C – H –

He realised the message had gone back to the beginning. It was repeating itself.

A – I – N – E – D – U – P – C – H –

He grouped the letters in his head.

CHAINED UP.

Sami wouldn't have thought it possible to be more scared. But he was. Was this Max or Lukas communicating with him? If he cut a hole in the hull, and they were chained to the vessel, he would kill them.

Unless he was able to free them before they sank.

That seemed to be his only option.

He fired up the welding unit with a flick of the ignition

trigger. A blindingly bright orange flame shot from the end of the lance, causing the water around it to bubble and boil furiously. It was loud enough to muffle the Morse code thudding. He touched the intense flame to the hull and was immediately surrounded by an impenetrable cloud of pulverised metal. The flame penetrated the hull almost immediately. He started to trace a circle, working as fast as the welding unit would allow.

Light.

It appeared just to the right of where Max was thumping his message on the inside of the hull, and it burned his vision. It was the tip of a flame, white hot and intense. It was immediately followed by a spurt of water jetting into the boat.

'They're here!' he shouted.

'What the . . . ?' Prospero was plainly astonished.

'We told you they'd come,' said Lukas.

The welding unit's flame arced upwards. Whoever was controlling it was moving quickly. The initial spurt of water became a jet, then a steady flow as the pressure from outside forced it into the hull.

'We're in here! We're chained!' Lukas shouted loudly, but Max knew there was no point. The water and the noise of the welding unit overpowered his voice. Max could just see Lukas's face, and Prospero's, by the light of the flame. They were shadowy and alarmed. Even Prospero was tugging at her chain in a futile attempt to loosen it.

By the time the welding unit had made a semicircle,

the water in the hull was ankle deep. Max, Lukas and Prospero were covered in spray. Lukas had stopped shouting. They were all banging on the hull, trying to attract the attention of the person with the welding unit.

They were silenced by a terrible creaking groan. The boat shifted in the water. The flame disappeared: its operator had been knocked back by the movement of the sinking vessel. It was totally dark again, but Max could hear the water gushing into the hole in the hull.

He was frozen with fear. He couldn't speak. He couldn't even move. He knew the ship was going down. In minutes, perhaps even in seconds, his nightmare about drowning would become a reality.

The barge was sinking much quicker than Sami expected. He'd only cut a semicircle in the hull. He knew he didn't have enough time to complete it. He had to work quickly. Instead of completing the circle, he started to cut across it. The water bubbled and billowed. The hull was still sinking but he kept at it, fiercely concentrating on keeping flame to metal. The line of his cut was jagged and uneven, but he had almost completed the semicircle . . .

Then the cut was complete. Sami extinguished the welding unit. The metal semicircle flew into the hull from the external pressure of the water, which gushed into the hole in a torrent. The boat sank a little more. Sami's every instinct screamed at him to get out of its way, to swim to the surface. But he couldn't. His job wasn't finished yet.

Sami cursed inwardly. The hole in the hull was too small

for him to squeeze through with his rebreather on. He'd have to ditch it. He unclipped it from his body and felt it float away. The welding unit, though, he kept strapped to his chest. He grabbed the edges of the semicircle and squeezed his way into the boat. The cutting apparatus scraped against the jagged edge of the metal, but within a few seconds he was in.

His head and shoulders were above water, but he couldn't see anything in the pitch black. He inhaled deeply, then shouted. 'Max? Lukas?'

His friends screamed back. He only heard parts of what they were saying. 'Sami . . . chained up . . . get out . . . save yourself . . .'

Sami ignited the welding unit again, more for light than heat. The angle of the sinking boat was such that Max and Lukas were neck-deep. Beyond Max was a third person – a woman with a bruised, leathery face. Their eyes were dead with terror. They shouted at him, but he couldn't understand them and there was no time to try.

Lukas was the closest. Sami gulped another lungful of air and dived towards him.

The water glowed, burnt orange. It had covered his mouth. Max stretched his neck upwards to suck in a final, desperate mouthful of air.

Then he was under.

The deafening roar of the water gushing into the boat became muffled, hardly there at all. He could see the welding unit glowing underwater, and the blurred silhouettes of

Sami and Lukas. Within seconds, Sami had freed Lukas, cut through his chain. They surfaced for oxygen. Max tried to do the same, but he couldn't: his chain wasn't long enough for him to reach the tiny pocket of air above. He looked at where Prospero had been. She was underwater!

His lungs were on fire. He started to panic. He needed air. He *had* to have it. His chest felt as though it would implode.

Then Sami was there. The welding unit was still burning, but to Max's horror he saw it flicker. Would there be enough fuel to cut through his chain? And what about Prospero's?

He felt dizzy. All of a sudden he was only half aware of his friend. He was desperate to inhale, even if it meant sucking in a lungful of river water . . .

Suddenly he felt the chain release. He urged himself upward, his body shrieking for oxygen. But the air pocket was no longer there. They were completely underwater!

He felt his blood pounding. Time seemed to slow down. He didn't know where he was or where to go. Then he felt somebody tugging his left arm. He allowed himself to be dragged through the water. It felt thick, like treacle. He could barely move.

Sharp metal. He was being squeezed through a hole with jagged edges that cut into his wetsuit. It was totally black, and he was alone. There was nobody with him any more. He knew, in the tiny corner of his mind that wasn't blanketed from lack of oxygen, that he had to get to the surface within seconds, or he'd die.

But which way should he swim?

It was like floating in space. There were no directions.

No up and down. Maybe, he thought, he should give up, let the overpowering drowsiness that had crept up on him simply take over . . .

No. The urge to survive kicked in and he realised what he had to do. He exhaled, feeling in front of his face for the bubbles, because they would always float to the top. He realised he was upside down. He righted himself and powered after them with all the strength he could muster. It took everything he had: the sinking barge had created an undertow that threatened to drag him deeper. With difficulty, he broke the surface of the water.

He had never gasped so hungrily and noisily for air – huge, reviving chestfuls of sweet oxygen. The dizziness and drowsiness disappeared. He wiped river water from his eyes and checked his surroundings.

He could just see the tip of the barge's stern. There were people in the water, splashing frantically. Some of them were shouting in Korean. They were obviously frightened, too concerned with saving their lives to pay any attention to the cadets. They were trying to swim to the bank.

All except two. Abby was next to him. She had removed her mask and her face was a picture of panic as she tried to stay afloat. Lukas was just beyond her. He had obviously broken the surface a little after Max, because he was still gasping for breath.

'Where's Sami?' Abby shouted. Her voice was unusually high-pitched and stretched. '*Where is he?*'

Max spun around, kicking hard to keep his face above the water. He could still feel the chain manacled to his ankle as he desperately searched for his friend. There was no sign of him – or of Prospero.

The boat had completely disappeared. The only sign of it was the swirling ripples and whirlpools it had left on the surface of the river, and the terrible undertow that felt like it would pull Max down.

'Where is Sami?' Abby shouted. Max's head felt like an echo chamber, her voice reverberating inside.

Where is Sami?

Where is Sami?

WHERE IS SAMI?

18

Searchlight

The instant Lili ended the call to Abby, she and Hwan started to run. And they hadn't stopped since.

They kept to the shadows wherever possible. The camouflage of trees. Along high walls. In one way it was like running through a ghost town. The ordinary citizens of Pyongyang were all in bed. Few civilians were about, and those who were walked hurriedly with their heads down and their shoulders hunched. In other ways, it was like a war zone. Helicopters buzzed overhead, flying north. Police sirens screamed in the distance. Lili and Hwan followed the line of the river, but not always directly. Hwan knew the city well. He was able to take them on routes that kept them away from the main road by the river. When they heard a siren close by, or a helicopter searchlight threatened to illuminate them, he was able to find a doorway, or a side street, or a thicket for them to hide in. As they passed the next bridge, they were sweating, scratched and sore. Lili checked the time: 03:20 hours. She felt dizzy with panic. They only had forty minutes left, and they were still on the wrong bank of the river.

'We need to get to one of the bridges,' Lili said as they

crouched, breathless, behind a bush on the edge of an immaculate public park. 'We need to cross the river.'

'The bridges are often guarded,' Hwan said. 'Tonight especially . . .' He looked steadily at Lili. 'Will they keep their word?'

'Who?'

'The British, of course. Will they keep their word about my parents?'

Lili didn't know. But she nodded firmly. 'I'm certain they will.' She wasn't sure Hwan believed her.

'The nearest bridge is Chongnu Bridge. It crosses an island in the middle of the river, then goes over to the other bank. Like the bridge over the hotel island.'

'How far is it?'

'Five minutes from here, if we run.' As he spoke, there was another siren in the distance. They froze and waited for it to fade away.

'I wish I knew how the others are getting on,' Lili said. 'I've got a bad feeling.'

'Call them,' said Hwan.

Lili nodded. She took out her sat phone and dialled Abby's number.

'*Where is Sami?*'

The Korean guards, saving themselves, were halfway to the shore. The water was still swirling. The undercurrents were strong. It was all Max could do to keep his head above water. He was woozy, and his body ached from the beating he had received on the boat. But he, Abby and Lukas continued to tread water, searching for some sign of their friend. There was none. A cold, sick feeling spread through Max's tired limbs.

There was a splash. A figure broke the surface close to Max. Max squinted through the darkness as he heard the heavy rasping sound of somebody inhaling desperately. He swam towards the sound, aware of Abby and Lukas doing the same.

'Sami?' he called. Then, when he realised it wasn't his friend, 'Prospero?'

Prospero was gulping in air and couldn't speak immediately. Max swam so he was face to face with her. 'Where is he? Where's Sami?'

'I don't know,' Prospero gasped. 'The last time I saw him . . . in the hull . . . cutting me free . . .'

'You didn't help him get out?' Max demanded fiercely.

'Lost each other . . .' she rasped. She seemed unable to get any more words out. Max wanted to shriek at her. How dare she leave Sami? How dare she not help him?

But his thoughts were broken by another splash. He spun round to see a second figure breaking the surface just behind him. Another almost inhuman gasp for air . . .

Sami.

His eyes rolled. His mouth and nose sank beneath the water. Max surged through the water and grabbed him from behind, keeping him afloat and his face exposed to the air.

'Talk to me!' he hissed. But Sami couldn't. After the initial intake of air, he could barely breathe.

'We need to get to the far side of the river,' Max shouted at the others. 'Quickly!'

Lukas was next to him, helping to keep Sami afloat. 'We do it together,' he said. Max didn't argue. He did his best to ignore the chain manacled to his ankle as they held one of Sami's arms each and powered through the turbulent water towards the river bank. Unhindered by Sami's weight, Prospero and Abby were able to move faster, but they kept close to Max and Lukas, ready to take over if they needed to.

They didn't. It was slow and exhausting work and the far bank approached only imperceptibly. But Max and Lukas found a rhythm. Before long, Max's feet touched cold, sludgy silt and they were able to carry Sami on to a shingle beach. A huge billboard overlooked the bank, showing a smiling picture of Kim Jong-un.

'Put him on his front,' Prospero said. Max wanted to argue with her, but he caught the expression on her bruised, swollen face and realised she knew what she was talking about. He rolled Sami over. Prospero slapped him hard between the shoulder blades, and an astonishing amount of river water gushed from his mouth.

'He's not breathing,' she said. 'Get him on to his back.'

Max rolled him over again. Prospero put her lips to Sami's and gave him two long rescue breaths. She got ready to start chest compressions, but Sami suddenly coughed and inhaled. His eyes flickered open and more water spilled from his mouth.

'Thank God,' Prospero said. 'We owe this one our lives.'

'You don't have to tell me that,' Max muttered. For some reason, he still felt an overwhelming anger towards Prospero.

'Hey,' Abby said. 'Who's this?' She pointed at Prospero.

'It's Prospero,' Max said.

If Abby felt surprised that Prospero was a woman, she didn't show it. She just carried on speaking with calm efficiency. 'Lili's managed to dupe the North Koreans. They think we're heading north. Hwan's parents are in a prison camp and we're going to demand their release in return for the two North Korean spies. We need to get to the pick-up zone by 04:00 hours.' She checked her watch: 03:30 hours. 'We only have thirty minutes. Remember, they said it was a disused football stadium two miles south of Pyongyang.'

'I know it,' said Prospero. 'But we're going to need a vehicle to get there in time.'

'How do we find one?' Abby said.

'Leave that to me. We need to get away from the river before they come searching for us. Let's move.'

'Wait,' Abby said. 'Lili and Hwan. We need to hook up with them first.'

'What's Hwan doing with Lili?' Max said.

'There isn't time to explain,' Abby said. As she spoke, her sat phone rang. She removed it from the pouch in her wetsuit and answered. 'Go ahead,' she said. And then: 'Wait, I'm going to put you on speaker.'

She pressed a button and Lili's voice became audible.

– *Are you safe?*

Abby looked round at the others: at Sami, kneeling, gasping and coughing. At Max and Lukas, bent double with exhaustion. At Prospero, who looked like she'd just come out of the ring with a heavyweight boxer. All of them dripping with river water and bedraggled.

'We're alive, if that's what you mean,' she said. 'Max, Lukas and Prospero are with us. The barge has gone down and we're on the other side of the river. Where are you?'

– *We're heading to Chongnu Bridge. We need to cross it.*

'It's five minutes in a vehicle,' Prospero said. 'Fifteen on foot.'

– *Who's that?*

'Prospero,' Abby said. 'We're going to find a vehicle. We'll meet you on the far side of Chongnu Bridge. Then we'll head to the . . .'

Abby stopped mid-sentence. Max knew why. From their position on the river bank, they were looking towards north Pyongyang. In the distance they could see three helicopters. They were heading their way.

'Lili,' Abby said tensely.

– *I see them.*

'You said the authorities thought we were heading north,' Lukas said accusingly.

'Yeah,' Abby replied. 'I guess having their prison boat on the river bed is making them think twice.'

– *Get moving.*

Lili hung up. The cadets and Prospero stared at the helicopters. Powerful searchlights beamed down over them, dancing crazily over Pyongyang. They were moving quickly in their direction.

Prospero picked up a sharp, heavy stone from the river bank. 'Can you walk?' she asked Sami, feeling the stone's weight.

Sami nodded shakily. Max helped him to his feet. They

staggered away from the river towards an area of rough scrub leading to a deserted main road. Moving was difficult with the chains manacled to their ankles. They were heavy and scraped along the ground behind them. Along the opposite pavement ran a perfectly straight line of trees, clearly intended to be attractive. Beyond them, though, was a run-down administrative building, several storeys high but with no lights on, its concrete façade cracked and crumbling. 'There's a car park behind of that building,' Prospero said. 'Let's get there. *Run!*'

Max kept one of Sami's arms over his shoulders and helped him across the road, following the others. They could still hear the helicopters. When he looked back towards the glowing lights of central Pyongyang, Max saw they were circling over the river, around the point where the barge had gone down. Searchlights were scanning the water. Max doubted that he and the others even had a minute before the choppers started to search this area.

'Come on, buddy,' he urged Sami. 'We need to up it.'

Sami nodded. They had crossed the road and were in the moon-shadow of the administrative building, shivering in their damp diving gear. Prospero led them along beside the building, her chain scraping along the pavement, still carrying the stone she'd found. When a vehicle moved along the road, headlights burning, she lay flat on the ground until it passed. The cadets did the same. Back on their feet, they hurried round to the rear of the building. Here there was a mural of fierce North Korean soldiers brandishing pistols. But there was a car park – of sorts. Cracked tarmac. A security booth with a broken window. Max could tell that this was a part of Pyongyang that tourists weren't supposed to see. There were only three vehicles here: a saloon car and two vans. One of the vans was much older than the others, dented and rusty. To Max's surprise, this was the van to which Prospero led them.

'Hey,' Abby called out. 'Shouldn't we use the other one?'

Curtly, Prospero shook her head, but left it to Lukas to explain. 'It's easier to hotwire older cars,' he said.

Prospero was already moving round to the front passenger door. 'Stand back,' she said. She pressed the stone against the bottom right-hand corner of the window. 'Top tip,' she said. 'It's much easier to break a window at the corner. It's weaker there and the frame of the window stops your hand following through into the broken glass.' With a sudden, sharp movement, she jabbed the stone into the corner of the window. She was obviously very strong. The glass shattered and fell into the passenger seat. Prospero unlocked the vehicle from the inside and clambered over the shattered glass to the driver's seat. 'Get into the back,' she shouted.

The others pushed the passenger seat forward and clambered into the van. Max saw Prospero rip off a panel under the steering wheel and grab a fistful of coloured cables. Seconds later, the engine coughed and started.

'Hold on!' she barked.

The cadets crouched on the bare floor of the van, keeping their heads lower than the windows so they wouldn't be seen. As Prospero hit the accelerator, they slumped together in the middle of the floor.

The van sped away from the car park. Max checked the time. 03:40 hours. Sweating through his damp dive gear, he knelt and checked out of the window. The helicopters with their searchlights were swarming over the river bank they had just vacated. They had to head for Chongnu Bridge to hook up with Lili and Hwan. Max's heart thudded at the thought of what the next twenty minutes would have in store.

19

Full 180

Hwan was not as fit as Lili. He bent double, gasping for air, as they stood beneath a sprawling tree looking towards Chongnu Bridge. The stretch of street they were on was tree-lined. Bunting with scores of tiny individual North Korean flags criss-crossed between the trees. Through the bunting they saw three helicopters circling over the river, their searchlights playing on the water. A few vehicles were crossing the bridge, but they did not appear to be police or military. Just civilian.

If they were going to cross, now was the time.

Lili took out her sat phone and dialled Abby. 'Where are you?'

– We're on our way. We're in an old white van. Prospero is driving. We're heading for the bridge.

'We're going to cross now,' Abby said, and hung up. She pulled Hwan up to standing. 'Come on. We can't wait. Look confident, as if you're supposed to be here.'

Hwan swallowed hard and nodded. They locked arms and strode across a main road, waiting to let a car pass. Hwan couldn't take his eyes off the circling helicopters, but Lili focused on their more immediate surroundings. The other side of the bridge was not visible in the darkness, but the way ahead – a pavement adjacent to the road – was clear. There were no other pedestrians, and – crucially – no police.

Lili kept her head, and her pace, up. She felt like she was dragging Hwan in her wake. So much for looking confident, she thought. She checked back over her shoulder. There was nobody following. Up ahead, their path was clear.

The helicopters had moved to the far bank of the river, their searchlights beaming down. Hwan kept looking at them, plainly terrified.

'It's okay,' Lili reassured him. 'As long as they're searching that area, it means they don't know where we are. Come on – we're almost at the island.'

And they were. To their left there was a large circular building that spanned the width of the island. To their right, open ground. They pressed forward, crossing the island in a couple of minutes. Now they were over the water again. Lili peered forward, desperate for the sight of an old white van up ahead. But there was no sign of it.

'Where are you?' Lili whispered. 'Where are –'

The shouts came as if from nowhere. Lili's heart sank. She and Hwan stopped, stock-still. Then they turned to peer through the darkness behind them. Hwan muttered something in Korean under his breath. Lili counted the figures: eight, maybe nine. They were on the bridge behind Lili and Hwan, and running towards them.

'*Run!*' Lili hissed. Her arm still linked with Hwan's, she started to sprint, dragging Hwan with her. The shouting grew louder. Lili knew she had to up her pace, but with Hwan slowing her down, that was impossible. It crossed her mind that she should let go of him, that she should run ahead and save herself. But she couldn't – wouldn't – do that. They had a deal. 'Keep running!' she shouted at him. 'As fast as you –'

There was a bang. She felt a rush of air just past her right ear. At first she didn't know what it was. But it was as if her instincts were several steps ahead of her conscious thoughts, because she was already flinging herself and Hwan to the ground. She understood what had happened: someone had just fired a gun at her. As they landed in a heap on the hard ground, a second shot rang out. She heard the bullet whizzing just above them. If they had still been running, that round would have slammed straight into one of them. Whoever had fired it was shooting to kill.

She rolled on to her back and looked towards the gunmen. They were getting closer. A third gunshot rang out. Hwan whimpered.

With trembling hands, Lili felt for her own pistol, the one she had stolen from room 1313 and which she had used to force Hwan from the hotel. She hadn't seriously considered that she might have to use it. Now, she realised, she had little choice. Shakily, she cocked the weapon and flicked the safety switch to semi-automatic. The gunmen were thirty metres away and closing. They were wearing military uniform. They were fast and fit.

She fired.

She had aimed the round above the heads of the advancing men. It was a warning shot, no more. But it worked. The soldiers immediately hit the ground, just as Lili and Hwan had done, and fell silent. Lili released a second round. The men stayed low and there was no immediate retaliation, but she and Hwan were outnumbered and outgunned. The advancing soldiers would realise that soon enough. When that happened, they had no chance.

Their only hope was the rest of the cadet force. Lili fumbled desperately for her sat phone. One-handed, her sweaty thumb slipping on the keypad, she dialled.

Prospero was driving soberly. Max understood why: a carefully driven vehicle was much less likely to attract attention. But it felt impossibly slow. He suppressed the urge to shout at her to drive faster.

Abby had removed a hairpin from her hair and unlocked the manacle round Lukas's ankle. She was just getting to work on Max's when her sat phone rang, the handset lighting up the back of the van. She answered it immediately and put the speaker phone on.

The first sound they heard was unmistakable: gunshot.

'What's happening?' Abby demanded.

– Get here quickly. We're under fire!

'What's your location?' Max shouted.

– We're on the bridge. We're pinned down with approximately eight soldiers shooting at us.

There was more gunfire.

They're firing again. Get here NOW!

'Did you hear that?' Max yelled at Prospero.

'Hard not to,' Prospero shouted back. She sounded calm,

but she put her foot down and the van sped up. They heard more gunfire over the phone line.

Max checked his watch. 03:45 hours. Only fifteen minutes until they needed to be at the pick-up zone. 'How much longer?' he shouted.

'Thirty seconds, maybe a minute.'

'That's too long!'

'We're on our way!' Abby shouted into the phone. 'Hold on, we're on our way!'

– Hold on, we're on our way!

If Abby sounded panicked, it was nothing compared to how Lili felt. The soldiers were still on the ground, but they had started to return fire. Their aim was not good. Like Lili, they were clearly shooting with handguns and the distance was too great for accurately aimed shots. But they were within range and as the sixth, seventh and eighth shots whizzed past them, Lili realised it was only a matter of time before one of them got lucky.

She had fired two shots herself and she didn't know how many rounds remained. She fired again, above the heads of the soldiers. She heard them shouting to each other. There was a brief pause in their return fire. Then it started up again.

'The helicopters!' Hwan shouted. 'They're coming this way! They know it is us!'

Lili swore. 'How much longer?' she shouted, and released another round over the soldiers' heads.

– We're on the bridge! We're twenty seconds away. Can you hold out that long?

'We don't have much choice,' Lili muttered under her breath, and released another two rounds in quick succession.

'Hold on tight!' Prospero bellowed. 'I can see them!' They were speeding along the bridge, the engine of the old van screaming. 'I'm going to make a handbrake turn. You'll be thrown around. As soon as I've turned, open the side door to let them in. We're going to draw fire, so keep yourself protected!'

But there was nothing in the van for them to hold on to, apart from each other. Max, Abby, Lukas and Sami interlocked their arms and gripped hard, ready for the speeding vehicle to spin a full 180.

Abby heard the vehicle before she saw it: the high-pitched whine of a struggling old engine speeding from the other end of the bridge towards them. From her prone position she saw its headlights approaching. 'Get ready to move!' she told Hwan as two more rounds narrowly missed them.

'Move?' Hwan whispered. 'We can't.'

'Fine,' Lili said. 'Lie here and let them take you. I'll say hi to your parents.'

'All right,' Hwan hissed.

Lili looked back again. The sound of the vehicle was getting louder. It was thirty metres away.

Twenty.

Ten.

She aimed her handgun above the heads of the soldiers again, ready to give covering fire.

'Get ready,' she hissed. 'In three, two, one . . .'

'Get ready!' Prospero shouted. 'In three, two, one . . . Now!'

She hit the brakes and spun the steering wheel. The cadets tumbled into each other. Max winced – his shoulder had crashed against hard metal. The tyres screeched as the vehicle twisted through 180 degrees before coming to a sudden halt.

'Open the door!' Prospero bellowed, but she didn't need to. Lukas had thrown himself against the side door and had yanked it open. There was gunfire, and Max tried to see what was happening through the opening. A round hit the chassis of the vehicle. They flung themselves away from the door, with not a second to spare. A second round entered the vehicle. It hit the interior of the van with a spark, then ricocheted to the floor only a few centimetres from Abby.

The vehicle was straining, a stone in a catapult ready to fly as soon as Lili and Hwan entered the van.

But there was no sign of them. *Where were they?*

'Go!' Lili shouted.

She fired three rounds in quick succession over the heads of the soldiers. Then she pulled Hwan to his feet and together they sprinted to the van. It was only about fifteen metres, but it felt a lot further. The van's door was shut. Her three rounds suppressed the soldiers' fire only for a couple of seconds. Lili and Hwan were ten metres from the vehicle when they fired again. The door slid open. A bullet hit the vehicle with a high-pitched metallic sound. A second round passed just by Lili's right ear and flew into the van.

She knew it was going to happen. The gunfire was too fast and too heavy for her to avoid it. When the bullet hit her, it felt like a solid thump on her right arm, followed by a flash of white-hot pain. It knocked her to the ground. Hwan, who was running next to her, somehow became caught up with her and fell too.

She felt blood oozing from her arm. The pain was sharp. Stabbing. Blinding.

'Get into the van,' Lili hissed at Hwan through clenched teeth. 'Leave me here.'

'Is that supposed to be a joke?'

Hwan grabbed her by her good arm and pulled her to her feet. Together they stumbled towards the van and Hwan pushed Lili inside. She collapsed on to the floor, bleeding badly but relieved to see her fellow cadets.

'Make sure Hwan gets in,' she whispered through the pain. But Lukas was already pulling him into the van.

'Go!' Max shouted. 'Prospero! Go!'

The van shot forward. Lili cried out in pain as one of the other cadets, she couldn't tell who, knocked against her arm. The sound of gunfire receded as somebody slid the door shut. It was dark inside. The cadets were talking at Lili, but she couldn't understand them. The pain in her arm was too intense. She clutched her arm. It was warm and sticky. She felt faint.

The vehicle accelerated. One of the cadets wrapped something tightly around Lili's arm. She didn't know who it was. Then the van suddenly filled with light, and she saw it was Abby. The cadets had fallen silent, and Lili knew why. Where was this new light coming from?

The vehicle turned dark, then light again. Then Max said what Lili was beginning to suspect. 'It's a searchlight! It's coming from one of the helicopters! They must know it's us! They're following! Prospero, we need to get to the pick-up zone! Now!'

20

04:00 hours

Max pressed his face against the van window. They had cleared the bridge. The soldiers who had been firing at Lili and Hwan were no longer in sight. From the back of the white van, Max could see two helicopters flying close and low, their searchlights beaming directly at the cadets' van. They had bigger problems.

'How far to the pick-up zone?' he asked Prospero.

'Ten minutes, if we don't hit a road block.'

'*What?*'

'How's that girl?' Prospero asked.

'She's losing blood,' Abby said. 'I've bandaged it and I'm putting pressure on the wound, but she needs help.'

'Then let's hope your friends turn up,' Prospero said.

She was clearly an expert driver. They moved at great speed through the suburbs of Pyongyang, Prospero controlling the old van as if it was a racing car. But it was impossible to outrun the two helicopters. They stuck terrifyingly close, their searchlights following the van so accurately that it was as bright as day in its interior. Max saw Abby tending Lili, her hands smeared with blood, her face intent. Sami was too exhausted from his exploits in the river even to look scared. Lukas was frowning, frustrated at his inability to do anything but crouch in the back of the van while Prospero did all she could to get them all to safety.

And Hwan. Max had last seen him at the hotel. Could it really have only been a few hours ago? Hwan was watching him, his expression impossible to read. As they stared at each other, Max became aware of something: sirens, distant but approaching. He snapped back to the situation outside.

'We've got police cars chasing us!' he warned Prospero over the engine.

Prospero said nothing. Max slid heavily against the side of the van as it turned sharply, and was dazzled by one of the searchlights beaming directly in his face.

Time check: 03:57 hours.

'How much further?' he yelled.

'Two minutes, maybe three. But don't expect this to be straightforward . . .'

'You don't say,' Max muttered. Through the rear window he could see the police cars, their blue neon lights urgent and close. He counted five, but knew there could be more.

'Abby! Throw me your sat phone!'

Abby did as he asked. Max dialled the number for the Watchers, but it didn't connect. He swore under his breath. They were just going to have to pray their pick-up would arrive.

'This is it!' Prospero called over her shoulder. Max checked out of the window, squinting against the searchlights but also using them to view the surrounding area. When the Watchers had said that the pick-up zone was a deserted football stadium, he had imagined Wembley. This place couldn't be more different. The van was speeding over a derelict pitch strewn with weeds and pot holes. There were grandstands at either end but one had collapsed in the middle. This place plainly hadn't been used for sport for many years. He looked up at the sky. The Watchers had said they would arrive in a stealth helicopter. He saw no sign of anything.

'Where are they?'

Nobody had an answer. Prospero urged the van to one end of the pitch and shouted, 'Hold on tight!' She performed another 180-degree handbrake turn so that she was facing the oncoming vehicles.

The van was still, the engine quiet. Although they could still faintly hear helicopters and sirens, it was weirdly silent. Max clambered over his fellow cadets to look through the front windscreen.

What he saw chilled him.

There were six police cars. They had stopped in a neat row, lights flashing, along where the halfway line should be. Behind them, the two helicopters were touching down. The headlights from the cars and the helicopters lit up the pitch in front of them, and Max could see the silhouettes of armed figures – ten, maybe more – stepping forward in a line in front of the police cars, before kneeling in the firing position.

Prospero was still gripping the steering wheel. She revved the engine, but the vehicle didn't move.

Time check: 03:59 hours.

'Where *are* they?' Max repeated. 'What do we do now?'

'Open the back of the van,' Prospero said quietly, her voice hoarse.

'But they're not . . .'

'Just do it, Max. Use the van as cover. Keep low. They're going to open fire any second. The van is our only cover.'

'What about you?'

Prospero's eyes narrowed. 'We do what we have to do,' she said. 'Stealth or not, your chopper can't land or take off without a distraction.' She turned to Max. 'I'm that distraction.'

'No,' Max told her. 'Wait –'

But as he spoke, a shot rang out from the police line. A round hit the windscreen. It didn't shatter, but a spiderweb network of cracks spread across the glass, making it impossible to see through. Prospero shouted, '*DO IT!*'

Lukas fumbled for the latch that opened the rear doors of the van. He opened them gingerly, as if expecting gunmen to be behind the vehicle as well as in front of it. But there was open ground: just a patch of weed-strewn football pitch and the rusted, misshapen frame of an old goal. Max checked his watch. It was 04:00 exactly. 'Where are they?' he muttered. 'Where the . . .'

He saw it, but he didn't hear it. A sleek, insect-like black helicopter appeared, slowly descending. Any sound from its rotor blades was masked by the growl of the van's idling engine. Its nose was pointing towards the back of the van, and it was so close that Max could see the pilot's face. The stealth helicopter was using the vehicle as cover.

'*Go!*' Prospero roared. 'Get to the chopper before they advance! Get out before they open fire!'

The cadets didn't argue. Lukas and Abby helped Lili out of the van. She was barely conscious and it took both of them to help her stagger towards the helicopter, which was open. Sami seemed disorientated, but could walk, just. He followed the others to the chopper.

That just left Max and Hwan.

Hwan had his back against the side of the van. Max stared at Prospero as if suddenly understanding something.

'*Get him out of here!*' Prospero roared, her voice shaking.

'*Go!*' Max hissed.

'I don't want her to . . .'

'*JUST GO!*'

Hwan swallowed hard. He ran to the back of the van and sprinted to the helicopter.

'You still there, Max?' Prospero called. She was revving the engine aggressively. 'Bad place to be.'

'Come with us!' Max shouted. 'You don't have to do this.'

'None of us *have* to do any of this. But as soon as that helicopter leaves the ground, those gunmen are going to open up. Stealth Black Hawk. Nice bit of kit. But a single round in its fuselage will ground it. Our friends with the firearms are going to need something else to shoot at. A van heading towards them at 70 mph should do it.'

'But they'll kill you if you do that.'

'And they'll kill *you* if I don't. I've been on borrowed time since they captured me, Max, and it just ran out. Now get the heck out of here before you mess the whole thing up.'

A strange smile crossed her face. 'It's the right thing to do.'

Max stared at her. All he could see was the reflection of her steely gaze. Like a bulletproof vest, she was impervious to arguments. He clambered to the back of the van, where he felt the fierce downdraught of the stealth chopper's rotor blades. He was about to jump out of the van when Prospero spoke again. 'Hey, Max!'

'What?'

'You and your friends are good. The best I've seen. Make sure you save a few lives for me, huh? You can start with the Korean kid's mum and dad.'

Max set his jaw. 'Roger that,' he said, and hurled himself from the van.

The rotor blades of the stealth chopper made a low *whomp*ing sound that seemed to be just on the edge of Max's hearing. There was the stench of burning rubber, and exhaust fumes billowed from the van as Max sprinted to the chopper and leaped inside. It was dark inside. He couldn't tell who was who, or where. He heard Hector's voice – '*GO GO GO!*' – and felt the helicopter lift up into the air. He spun round to see the door of the chopper closing. There was a small porthole window and he pressed himself up against it to look out at the scene below.

The van was speeding towards the line of armed men. They broke formation and scattered to escape it. The helicopter banked, and Max lost sight of the ground. A few seconds later, it straightened up and he could see again. The van had turned and stopped. Clearly Prospero never had any intention of hitting the gunmen.

Her compassion was not returned. As Max watched in horror, there was a barrage of muzzle flashes, crackling like sparklers all around the van. As Black Hawk continued to rise, Max had to strain his neck to keep the van in sight. He wished he hadn't. The entire van erupted into an orange and black fireball. He squeezed his eyes shut, but the fireball was burned on his retina and he could see it clearly for a full ten seconds before it faded away.

When he opened his eyes again, the ground was out of sight. Black Hawk had turned and was travelling faster. Exhausted, drained and sickened, he collapsed to the floor of the helicopter.

He knew Prospero was dead. Nobody could have survived an explosion like that. Everything they had gone through over the past twenty-four hours had been for nothing.

The operation had been a disaster. The Special Forces Cadets had failed.

21

DMZ

Max slumped inside the chopper. He was just aware of Lili whimpering with pain. Woody and Angel lifted her on to a stretcher bed that was fixed to the chopper. The other cadets crowded round them.

'Get to your seats!' Angel shouted. 'Don't get in our way!'

Reluctantly, the cadets moved to uncomfortable high-backed airline seats. Hwan was still crouching on the ground. He looked as if he might faint. Hector, with uncharacteristic gentleness, helped him into a seat. Then he turned and, grim-faced, indicated that Max should take a seat close to the flight deck. Hector consulted with Woody and Angel, then came and sat next to him.

'She's going to be okay. Lili, I mean. The bullet just grazed her arm. She's lost some blood and it's going to hurt for a bit, but –'

'How many cadets have died on operations?' Max interrupted.

'Enough,' Hector replied. It was clear he would say no more. After a brief pause, Hector spoke again. 'MH-X Stealth Black Hawk,' he said. 'Invisible to radar and any other location-searching devices the North Koreans might throw at it. We have a Special Forces flight crew.' He pointed at the two men in the flight deck who were navigating with the aid of night-vision goggles. 'Those two choppers back at the football ground might try to chase us, but they'll never catch us. We're heading straight to the South Korean side of the de-militarised zone. Once we're there, we're safe. The North Koreans won't risk a conflict beyond the DMZ.'

'We messed it up, didn't we?' Max said.

'What makes you say that?' Hector seemed genuinely perplexed.

'Our job was to rescue Prospero. Now she's dead.'

'Your job was to give Prospero a fighting chance. What she did with that chance was up to her.'

Max suppressed a wave of anger. Hector sounded cold and matter-of-fact. But he didn't look it. Max realised the older man's true feelings were perhaps more complex than he, Max, could understand.

'She didn't have a family, did she?' Max asked.

Hector didn't reply.

'You didn't want us to know her real name because you knew she might die in the rescue attempt. If we knew her real name, we'd have felt closer to her and found it more difficult if she died. You lied to us from the beginning.'

'There's a difference between lying, Max, and protecting you from the truth.'

Max didn't know what to say. They were silent again. 'She didn't have to do that,' he said eventually. 'We could have all got out alive. Including her.'

'Sure we could,' Hector said. 'This aircraft is fitted with

two 7.62 millimetre miniguns and a Hellfire missile. We could have taken out those North Korean gunmen in an instant, and the choppers. But how many men would we have killed? Ten? Fifteen? For obeying the orders of a regime that would kill them if they refused? Plus, by now the UK would be at war with North Korea.' He gave Max a hard stare. 'We'd have done it, Max. We'd have done it to get you cadets out of there. We'd have done it for Prospero too. She knew that. She decided that her way was better. For what it's worth, I admire her decision.'

'It doesn't seem fair.'

'Fair? Stop talking like a child. Of course it isn't fair. Life isn't fair. You know that.' He waved one arm to indicate the other cadets. 'You *all* know that. So remember it. You think every military operation goes the way we expect it to? You think this is a movie, where everything turns out okay in the end and we all ride off into the sunset? Nobody wins wars, Max. We just do what we think is right at the time. And we try to keep the body count down.' He looked at his watch. 'If everything goes according to plan, we'll cross the DMZ in a little less than an hour. Our work isn't over.' He nodded towards Hwan, who was clutching his knees and staring into the middle distance. 'Our superiors are speaking to the North Koreans about Hwan's parents. Something good can still come out of this.' He moved over to help Woody and Angel with Lili.

05:59 hours.

The sky was lightening before dawn when the Black

Hawk touched down. Abby had removed Max's manacle and chain, but his muscles were so exhausted he felt like he was still carrying it. Aching with tiredness, he stepped out. The landing zone was a wasteland. There were no buildings, and no people. This was a place where nobody came. A place where secret events could occur. They were on the south side of a high barbed-wire fence. Beyond it was the demilitarised zone – a rural landscape smothered in early-morning mist. The helicopter powered down. The cadets – minus Lili – stood in a circle, facing north, unsure what would happen next. Max could hear the sound of birdsong, the dawn chorus. He supposed that, in an area where humans were discouraged, animals could thrive. Hwan stood a little apart from them, staring towards his homeland, an inscrutable expression on his face.

'I guess he can never go back,' Sami said.

'Guess not,' Max agreed.

They heard the sound of an approaching helicopter and all turned to look at it.

'It's the spies,' Angel said, stepping out of Black Hawk. 'The ones the North Koreans wanted to exchange in return for Prospero. We've arranged for that helicopter to take you to a South Korean military base. You'll be safe there. We'll take it from here.'

'No.'

The cadets spoke in unison – even Lili, who had appeared from the chopper, her arm in a sling and her face drawn, but upright and conscious.

'No what?' Hector said, appearing next to her.

'We're staying here until we see that Hwan and his parents are reunited,' Lukas said.

'You think we'd lie to you about something like that?' Angel said.

'There's a difference between lying,' Max said, glancing at Hector, 'and protecting us from the truth. We're staying here.'

Hector and Angel exchanged a long look. Then Hector nodded. He disappeared back into the helicopter.

The chopper from the south touched down fifty metres from them. Four Korean men emerged. Two wore blue boiler suits and their wrists were cuffed. The other two wore military uniform. Heads bowed under the downdraught, they led the handcuffed men towards an area of open ground, firmly but not unkindly. The Koreans stared at the cadets but did not approach. The prisoners sat on the ground. Their guards knelt down in the firing position, their weapons pointing towards North Korea. The chopper powered down. There was silence.

The day passed slowly as they waited for the exchange to take place. The flight crew and the Watchers made and received occasional messages over Black Hawk's secure radio. The cadets recuperated. Lili was obviously in great pain, but she didn't complain and the cadets refrained from asking her how she felt. She spent most of the day lying on the stretcher bed in Black Hawk, with at least one cadet and a Watcher sitting with her. The rest of them paced impatiently outside, or slept uncomfortably in the aircraft seats. Only Hwan remained awake the whole time. Alone. Silent and unwilling to speak. Max couldn't imagine what was going through his mind. As the sun started to set, Max emerged from Black Hawk to find Hwan kneeling on the ground, his head in his hands. Max walked up to him. 'You okay?'

Hwan shook his head. 'They are not coming. I know it.'

Max was about to reassure him when he saw Woody and Angel approaching. Their faces were flinty and Max could tell they were bringing bad news. 'What is it?' he said.

'The North Koreans –' Woody said – 'they've just been in touch. They're furious that we breached their airspace, so they won't play ball. They have Hwan's parents, but they're refusing to make the trade. They –'

'What?' Hwan said sharply.

'I'm sorry, Hwan. They say they're going to execute your parents as punishment for your defection.'

Hwan stared at him. Then he put his face in his hands again and wept. Max felt sick. First Prospero, now this.

'No,' he said firmly. 'We can't let that happen.'

'We always knew it was a possibility, Max,' Woody said.

But Max was striding to Black Hawk. His blood was hot with anger. He could hear Prospero's voice in his head. *Make sure you save a few lives for me, huh? You can start with the Korean kid's mum and dad . . .*

He found Hector inside the aircraft. He was telling the flight crew to get ready to depart. Max pulled him away. 'Come with me,' he said. Hector looked outraged at being spoken to like that. But one glance at Max's face told him it was serious. Max led him outside to where the others stood. Woody had obviously just told them the problem.

'Do something about it,' Max said to Hector.

'You overestimate my influence, Max,' Hector said quietly.

'And you underestimate ours. Lili made Hwan a promise. We stand by it. It's . . . it's the right thing to do. If we leave here without Hwan's parents, you'll have their blood on your hands and you'll be in the market for a new team of Special Forces Cadets. Right, everyone?'

'Right,' the others said. Lili's voice was the loudest, despite her injury.

Max expected an argument from Hector, and he was up for the fight. He had his friends with him. But Hector was looking at him strangely. Respectfully. With pride, even. Woody and Angel joined them. They stood just behind Hector, staring at Max and the others.

Wordlessly, Hector removed a handset from his jacket. It was larger than the sat phone the cadets had been using, with a full-colour screen and a sturdy antenna. He dialled a number and spoke. 'Patch me through to the North Korean negotiating team,' he said. Then, *Just do it.*'

They stood in silence. The sun continued to set, turning the DMZ blood-red. Hector kept the handset to his ear. They waited.

A minute.

Two.

Finally Hector spoke. 'Can you hear me? Is there an interpreter on the line?' He waited for a reply, unheard by the cadets, then carried on. 'Late last night, a British team infiltrated Pyongyang, rescued a prisoner from a prison boat, escaped a full team of police and military personnel and helped a young North Korean man to defect. I'd say that was a pretty bad night for a regime that prides itself on the strength of its military and its control over its people. I hope you're listening and watching carefully, because I'm going to show you the team that made your proud military seem like a bunch of amateurs.' He tapped the screen of his phone and held it up. Max realised he was sending a photo of the cadets.

And as Hector held up the phone, Max looked at Lili, her arm in a sling but her chin jutting out defiantly. At Lukas, who appeared surlier and more aggressive than normal. At Abby, exuding a hint of cheerful arrogance, her head inclined and a spark in her expression. At Sami, plainly exhausted, with dark rings under his eyes, but as earnest as ever. And then down at himself, still in his diving gear, feeling cold now the sun was setting. Max was aware that he was part of a unit that must surely be a horror show for the North Korean negotiators watching them. Because although everything Hector had said about their night's work was true, there was one important fact he'd failed to mention. This was not a unit of hardened, grizzled soldiers with years of operational experience behind them. It was a bunch of teenagers, and they had survived everything the North Koreans could throw at them.

Hector tapped the screen and put the phone to his ear again. 'You have one hour to make the exchange. If you fail, we will leak the salient facts of this mission on to the internet. The world will know that the combined might of the North Korean military was not enough to stop five children. Try explaining that to your glorious leader. That's all I have to say.' He killed the call and put the phone back in his pocket. 'One hour,' he repeated. 'Then we leave.' He turned his back on the cadets to stare across the DMZ to the border.

It grew dark. The cadets stood in a line, facing north. Within half an hour their shadows had lengthened, then disappeared. Within forty-five minutes they were relying on the light of the moon to see through the barbed-wire fence and across the no man's land of the DMZ.

But there was nothing to see. No movement. No personnel. Just the trees and the hills surrounding the DMZ. Max sidled up to Hector. 'Is it bad they have our picture?' he asked. 'I mean, for future missions . . .'

Hector shrugged. 'They know what you look like anyway. You won't be able to operate in North Korea again. But if I'm right, the North Koreans will do everything they can to make sure that picture never sees the light of day.'

There was silence. Hwan had stopped weeping and was also staring across the DMZ with an expression that was half dread, half expectation.

Fifty minutes had passed since Hector had made the call. Fifty-five.

'They are not coming,' Hwan said. Max thought he was right. There was no sign of . . .

'What's that?' Sami said.

Max squinted through the darkness. At first he couldn't see anything, then he detected movement. The movement morphed into two figures. They were clutching each other, walking slowly, one with an obvious limp.

Hwan was trembling. 'Is it them?' Max asked.

Hwan didn't answer. He ran to the barbed-wire fence, clutched it and peered out across the DMZ at the people approaching them. A loud sob broke the silence. It came from Hwan. He shouted something in Korean. But the figures couldn't shout back. They were too old and tired and weak.

It took five more minutes for Hwan's mother and father to reach the fence. They looked ancient. Their faces were lined, their cheeks sunken and their shoulders stooped. It was Hwan's father who limped. He was also crying. Hwan's mother was silent, but her shoulders were shaking with emotion. Their clothes were dirty and torn. But when they saw Hwan waiting for them, it was as if the years fell away. They seemed to Max able to stand a little straighter and walk a little faster. At the fence they reached their frail hands through the wire to touch Hwan's face. But they could not embrace him through the fence. There was no way through.

The South Korean soldiers approached with their two prisoners. One of the soldiers had a chain cutter, much like the one Max had tried to take to Prospero. He used it to snip a vertical hole in the fence, which curled open. The old couple stepped through. Tearfully, they embraced their son. The soldiers uncuffed the two North Korean spies and allowed them to walk through the fence and out into the DMZ. As soon as they were free, the spies ran.

Sami's eyes were brimming, and the other cadets looked as if they weren't far from tears. The two South Korean soldiers started to usher Hwan and his parents towards their helicopter, but he broke away from them and jogged towards the cadets. He shook them all by the hand, lingering when he came to Lili. 'I do not know how to thank you,' he said.

'You already did,' Lili said. 'By helping us escape. That was brave.'

'Or stupid,' Hwan said with a rueful smile.

'No,' Angel cut in. 'Brave. There's a difference. Trust me.'

Hwan's parents were halfway to the helicopter. They had stopped and were looking back anxiously, still holding each other.

'Go,' Max said. 'Take care of them. And have a good life.'

Hwan nodded gratefully, then ran to his elderly mum and dad. The cadets watched him go. Max thought he could guess what they were thinking: that each of them would give anything for a miraculous reunion with their own parents. But that was never going to happen, because they had none. They were Special Forces Cadets for a reason.

Hwan and his parents had disappeared into the chopper, and its rotors were powering up.

'I don't know about you lot,' Angel said, 'but I've had about enough of this place. Come on. Let's load up. It's time to go home.'

Chris Ryan

Chris Ryan was born in Newcastle.

In 1984 he joined 22 SAS. After completing the year-long Alpine Guides Course, he was the troop guide for B Squadron Mountain Troop. He completed three tours with the anti-terrorist team, serving as an assaulter, sniper and finally Sniper Team Commander.

Chris was part of the SAS eight-man patrol chosen for the famous Bravo Two Zero mission during the 1991 Gulf War. He was the only member of the unit to escape from Iraq, where three of his colleagues were killed and four captured. This was the longest escape and evasion in the history of the SAS, and for this he was awarded the Military Medal. Chris wrote about his experiences in his book *The One That Got Away*, which was adapted for screen and became an immediate bestseller.

Since then he has written four other books of non-fiction, over twenty bestselling novels and three series of children's books. Chris's novels have gone on to inspire the Sky One series *Strike Back*.

In addition to his books, Chris has presented a number of very successful TV programmes including *Hunting Chris Ryan*, *How Not to Die* and *Chris Ryan's Elite Police*.

Want to read
NEW BOOKS
before anyone else?

Like getting
FREE BOOKS?

Enjoy sharing your
OPINIONS?

Discover

READERS FIRST

Read. Love. Share.

Get your first free book just by signing up at
readersfirst.co.uk

HOT KEY BOOKS

Thank you for choosing a Hot Key book.

If you want to know more about our authors and what we publish, you can find us online.

You can start at our website

www.hotkeybooks.com

And you can also find us on:

We hope to see you soon!